Laura Fitzpatrick.

Murtagh and the Vikings

'As the flames grew higher, the Vikings began
to load the two ponies with sacks full of
weapons, goblets, wine and meat which they
found in the hall. The weapons of the dead
guards were also collected, and, in a while, the
party turned back towards the beach. As they
reached the stunted wood, Murtagh turned
back. A column of smoke towered up from the
courtyard behind them and a number of large
black birds flew in from the countryside.

'The ravens are gathering,' said Erik
Redbeard. 'They always attend a funeral pyre
in my land. Perhaps they come now to take your
monk and king to Valhalla!'

Murtagh shuddered . . .'

Before him lies a stormy journey by longboat
to Norway. And after that, what will be his
fate? Murtagh and the Vikings *is a dramatic
and exciting story which brilliantly evokes the
world of the Vikings.*

Roger Chatterton Newman

Murtagh and the Vikings

Illustrated by Terry Myler

HAWTHORN BOOKS

The Children's Press

For Boo and his brothers

First published in 1986 by
The Children's Press
90 Lower Baggot Street, Dublin 2

© Text Roger Chatterton Newman
© Illustrations The Children's Press

ISBN 0 947962 05 0 paperboards
ISBN 0 947962 06 9 paper

Typesetting by Computertype Ltd.
Printed in Ireland by Mount Salus Press.

Contents

Illustrations

*The Rathlin Island in this book refers to Lambay Island,
off the coast of Dublin. Several writers identify the first
Viking attack with the Rathlin Island off the Antrim coast.
This is because both were anciently known as* Reachrainn
(which is how the annalists recorded the attack).

1   The Fury of the Northmen

It was a wild and stormy evening in the year of the Lord 795. Dusk had just fallen and young Murtagh was out on the hillside, looking for some sheep which had strayed. As he reached the top of the hill the wind grew stronger and rain began to fall. Shivering, he wrapped the woollen cloak that had been his father's closer around him, wishing he was back beside the open fire in his uncle's snug croft, where he had lived since his parents died when he was a baby.

On the other side of the hill the land fell towards the cliff edge and the sea. But there was no sign of the sheep.

'I hope the stupid creatures haven't gone too near the edge and fallen over,' he thought, as crouching against the wind and rain he made his way slowly down the slope. Still no sign! On hands and knees he edged forward cautiously towards the treacherous cliff edge and looked over. There were no fleecy bodies on the rocks below, but his sigh of relief was short-lived. There *was* something there, something which made him stare in amazement. Pulled up in the lee of the cliff, rocking on the foam-checked water, were five strange ships.

They were long, curved vessels, and even in the dusk Murtagh could see that the prows were carved in strange sinuous shapes, making him think of the serpents he had heard about from his friend Brother Padraig at the monastery, and which some men said lurked in the depths of the ocean. They were certainly

9

not at all like the boat his uncle and cousins used for fishing along the shore, which rode high in the waters.

Now Murtagh could see that there were men in the ships. Then came bursts of flame as torches were lighted, flames reflected in savage-looking axes. The men, whoever they were, were armed.

Suddenly Murtagh remembered a story he had heard — or rather overheard, when his elders thought he was not listening. In a subdued voice Brother Padraig had been telling Murtagh's uncle about the destruction of a monastery on the coast of Northumbria across the sea, and how many of the monks, friends of Brother Padraig, had been killed or carried off in long, curved boats. He remembered what Brother Padraig had called the raiders — the Land Leapers.

Even as he watched, Murtagh saw that the men were leaving the boats and were wading, knee-deep, towards the shore. The torchlight fell on the savage weapons, broad shields and the wild beards and hair of the strangers.

There was only one way up from the strand, a steep cliff path that led to where Murtagh was lying. As quickly as he could, he crawled backwards, away from the cliff edge, knowing that if he stood up the men would see him outlined against the cliff top. When the ships were hidden from view, he stood up and began to run. His home was not far away, one of the little crofts that were scattered about Rathlin Island, and as he ran through the wind-swept night, his heart beating, he wondered whether the little building of stone and thatch would be strong enough to protect his family from these men.

10

He looked over his shoulder. The land dipped here and he could see no sign of the strangers behind him. But they must surely have reached the cliff top by now! Was that a sudden flicker of light in the distance? Then another ... and another...

Breathless, Murtagh fell through the curtain of hide hanging across the doorway of his home. In the firelight he saw his uncle Aonghus, the fisherman, his aunt Orlaidh, and his young cousins Fionn and Cathal, mending the great nets they would use the next day.

'Why, Murtagh, you look as though you've seen a ghost,' said Aonghus. 'Did you find the sheep?'

'Uncle ... uncle ... quickly ...,' gasped Murtagh. 'They're here ... the Land Leapers ... great boats ... axes....'

Aonghus, a heavily-built man with black hair and beard and skin burned red by years of sun and salt-spray, stood up. He too was remembering Brother Padraig's dreadful tale of the Northumbrian monastery, and instantly took command of the situation.

'If they are coming from the strand, this is the first house on the way. We can't stay here, and we must warn the others. Fionn, you're a good runner. Go straight to our neighbours and tell them to collect any weapons and gather at the monastery. Quickly — we've only a few minutes!

'Murtagh, take your aunt to the monastery and tell Brother Padraig what has happened. I must see to the boats — Cathal, you come with me. We may have to get the women and children across to the mainland, and we don't want the boats to fall into the Land Leapers' hands.'

Orlaidh, her face white in the firelight, began gathering up the wooden platters and drinking vessels from the floor.

'There's no time for that,' said Aonghus urgently. 'Just wrap a warm cloak around you and go — at once!'

Murtagh took his aunt's hand and together they went out into the night. It had stopped raining, and stars were appearing in the sky. There was no sign of the Land Leapers, but Murtagh knew that they could not be far behind. They ran on, stumbling across the turf, all the time being joined by neighbours, the women hastily dressed and clutching children taken from their beds and still sleepy. Donal Mór, the strongest man on the island, appeared carrying three long javelins which he had used years ago when he had fought in the wars for the King of Meath.

'Where's your uncle, Murtagh?' asked Donal and, when Murtagh told him, he turned back. 'He'll need some help. If we can bring the boats around we will stand a better chance of getting the women and children off the island.'

The monastery was a collection of little stone and thatched huts where the monks lived, a small church built of the same material and, just outside the stone-walled enclosure, a tall bell-tower. The doorway to the tower was some way above the ground, because the building was also used as a storage place. When the monastery was founded over two hundred years before, there had been the fear of thieves crossing from the mainland. The high doorway ensured they couldn't get in unless they brought a ladder with them or found where the monks hid theirs.

The monks were just coming out of the church as Murtagh and the others came tumbling through the gate of the enclosure. Brother Padraig, a kindly man and a great favourite with the island children, acted quickly when he heard Murtagh's news.

'We must shelter in the tower,' he said. 'It's the only building without a thatched roof.'

Even as he spoke, shouts were heard in the distance and flames sprang into the night from the direction of Murtagh's home. Over the brow of the hill came a line of torches and Orlaidh cried out, 'Aonghus, Fionn, Cathal, where are they — they'll be trapped.'

'Quickly, aunt,' said Murtagh, 'go to the tower. Uncle and the others will be safe if they can get to the boats. Look — here's Fionn now.'

Fionn rushed through the gateway, followed closely by two or three other boys. All clutched a makeshift weapon of some sort — Fionn a stout pole, another a broken javelin, another a spear used for catching eels. Even in the moment of danger, Brother Padraig could not help smiling.

'I don't think boys will stand much chance against these visitors of ours,' he said. 'Help me with the ladder ... and then into the tower with you.'

Fionn turned red. 'I am fourteen,' he said, 'and can fight like any man.'

'So can I,' said Murtagh, 'and I'm only six months younger than Fionn.'

'No arguments,' said Brother Padraig. 'Now — to work!'

As the great ladder was hauled out from its hiding-place, more flames lit up the night.

'They're firing the houses,' cried an islander.

The frightened people waited while Brother Padraig and the boys placed the ladder in position and Murtagh scrambled up to open the door. One by one, the women and children climbed or were helped up the rungs into a small chamber, from which another ladder led higher into the tower.

'There's plenty of room,' shouted Murtagh to his aunt, who was helping the children. 'Go to the top!'

The line of torches was coming closer as the last of the women and children disappeared into the tower. Murtagh slipped down the rungs as he saw Brother Padraig and two of the monks staggering from the church with heavy bundles.

'Let me help you, Brother,' said Murtagh, shouldering one of the bundles — the few precious pieces of the monastery's plate wrapped up in cloaks.

Someone began to ring the bell.

'That will be Fionn,' said Murtagh. 'He's letting my uncle and the others know that we are in the tower.'

As the last bundle was pushed hastily through the doorway, and Murtagh, Brother Padraig and another monk began to pull the ladder upwards, the Land Leapers poured into the enclosure. There seemed to be forty or fifty or them, or so Murtagh judged by the torches, and almost at once the place was ablaze with light as the torches were flung on to the thatched roofs of the monks' cells. The invaders were fierce-looking men, their wild red hair and beards made redder by the fire-light. With savage cries, they turned to the church and then one of them saw the tower, where Murtagh and Brother Padraig were still struggling with the ladder.

'Stand back in there,' shouted Brother Padraig. 'Make more room — we must get the ladder up.'

'It's stuck!' yelled Murtagh.

Even as he spoke two of the raiders leaped the wall of the enclosure and ran towards the tower. One, a giant of a man, wearing a helmet decorated on each side with wings, swung at the end of the ladder with his axe. It caught, and Murtagh was nearly pulled from the doorway.

'Pull, pull, quickly!' screamed Brother Padraig, and other hands joined in to help.

By now both raiders were swinging at the ladder with their axes, and every time a blow fell, the people in the tower almost lost their balance. Looking round, Murtagh saw the weapons brought by Fionn and his friends lying on the chamber floor. He grabbed the eel spear, aimed it at the giant raider and, with all his might, threw. It struck the man on the shoulder, just as he was about to swing his axe again, knocking him off balance. With a curse, he dropped the axe, as, with a final heave, the islanders and monks pulled the ladder clear of the ground and into the tower.

Brother Padraig slammed fast the door and rammed the stout pole against it.

'That should keep them out,' he panted, 'but who's to know whether they have ladders on these ships of theirs. If only we had more weapons...'

Murtagh and Fionn clambered up the inside ladder to the top chamber and peered from the narrow windows. A terrible sight met their eyes! The roof of the little church was now burning furiously, and across the island stretched a chain of blazing fires. Several of the raiders

16

had bundles slung across their backs, having obviously looted whatever they found in the crofts before setting them alight. Others carried long poles between them, on which were slung sheep; Murtagh realized with a sinking feeling that his uncle's sheep must have been discovered after all. He hoped that his uncle, Cathal and Donal Mór had saved the fishing boats.

The giant raider at whom Murtagh had thrown the eel spear seemed to be the leader. Now he was calling the others around him. Murtagh could not hear his words, but saw that he was pointing at the tower. Suddenly, with harsh cries, the raiders turned towards it; the leader, protecting his head with a shield, rushed to the base, followed by two more who lifted him on to their shoulders. Murtagh saw the glint of the axe as the raider swung it against the bottom of the door. It stuck fast in the wood and immediately another raider flung the noosed end of a long rope towards it. He missed and the rope fell to the ground. But at the second throw the noose caught the axe and held fast. The raiders cheered as one of them began to climb up the rope towards the door.

There was a narrow ledge at the base of the doorway, and on this the raider placed his feet, at the same time taking hold of the heavy iron ring which served as a door handle. Then with his free hand he took the axe which hung at his waist, and with powerful swings began to attack the door. He was a strong man and the wood was old; very soon it began to splinter — and then the axe-head broke through the door and was caught.

This was the moment Brother Padraig had been waiting for. Quick as a flash, he swung the door back into the chamber, dragging with it the raider who was still holding the iron ring. Then, dealing the man a mighty blow with a pole, he sent him hurtling out on to the heads of his companions.

Frantically, Brother Padraig pulled the axe out of the door while Murtagh hauled up the length of rope. As they did so, another axe came cutting through the air into the chamber, luckily without hitting anyone.

Brother Padraig slammed the door shut.

'At least we have two real weapons now,' he said grimly. 'What will they try next, I wonder?'

As if in answer, there was a loud clap of thunder and a streak of lightning; then down came the rain in torrents. The people in the tower could hear the loud hissing noise it made as it fell on the burning roof of the church.

Murtagh ran to the narrow window.

'They're going, they're going,' he shouted, and indeed the raiders seemed to be moving off. Turning occasionally to shake their axes in the direction of the tower, they gathered up their plunder and the dead

sheep and moved away in the direction of their ships.

'We'll stay here till morning,' said Brother Padraig. 'Brother Lorcan and I will keep watch, the rest of you try to sleep. There is a bitter and busy day ahead of us. As soon as it's light, one of us must go across to the mainland and tell our brothers at the monastery of Duibhlinn what has happened. They will be able to send word to the High King, Aodh.'

'Do you think the Land Leapers will come back, Brother Padraig?' asked Murtagh after a while.

'I don't know, my son. I have heard that they have been raiding the coasts of Northumbria, in the land of the Saxons, for five or six years, and many good monks have lost their lives. They have never come to our land before, but I am frightened that what has happened to-night could be the start of many raids.'

'Will High King Aodh be able to beat them?' asked Murtagh, who had heard tales of this great ruler, head over all the kings in Ireland. He also knew that he had the nickname of *Oirdnidhe*, which meant 'fist sucker', and although he had never seen a king of any sort, he thought this a very strange thing for a grown man to do.

'The king has many problems,' said Brother Padraig. 'There are too many other princes who think that they should be the most powerful in the land, and don't like sending gifts, or paying tribute as it is called, to King Aodh.'

'Does King Aodh live near the monastery of Duibhlinn?' asked Murtagh, who was now beginning to feel sleepy. He lay on the floor of the upper chamber, his head resting on one of the bundles brought from the church.

19

'No, my son,' chuckled Brother Padraig. 'Duibhlinn is only a little monastery, not much bigger than our own, near the ford of the hurdles. King Aodh lives in a great fort called the Grianan of Aileach, away in the north of the mainland; but he often comes to Duibhlinn on his journeys around Ireland.'

Murtagh woke next morning as the daylight came through the narrow windows. At first he wondered where he was, and then the events of the night flooded back. The monks had already lowered the ladder and the islanders were standing in the enclosure, looking with sad eyes at the damage. Everywhere was covered with blackened water-logged thatch, which now steamed as the rays of the sun touched it.

'At least no lives have been lost,' said Brother Padraig, 'but I wonder what's happened to Aonghus and Donal Mór.'

A little later, Murtagh, on look-out, saw a lone figure approaching. It was Cathal, his cousin, who had gone with Aonghus and Donal Mór to secure the boats.

Orlaidh ran to him. 'Cathal, thank goodness you're safe, but where's your father ... and what's happened to your arm?' Cathal's left arm was roughly bandaged and there was a spot or two of dried blood on his cheek. He looked tired.

'Father's safe, but Donal Mór is badly hurt,' he said. 'We reached the boats and were about to push them out when four Land Leapers came from nowhere. They must have been sent to see whether there were any boats on the island. Donal Mór killed one with the first thrust of his javelin. Father got another. Then Donal slipped,

20

and the third one caught him with his axe. Father finished that fellow off, and as for the fourth ... well, I got him with one of Donal's javelins.

'Donal was unconscious by then, so we had to put off in two boats. We managed to beach them in the next bay, but we couldn't move because of Donal. We heard the bell ringing, and knew you must have reached the tower.'

'Did you see any sign of the longboats, at all?' asked Brother Padraig.

'Not a sign,' said Cathal, 'but every croft I passed has been burned. Father said you should get down to Donal as soon as you can.'

'I know what I'll do,' said Murtagh excitedly. 'I'll go up to where I saw the boats last night, and see if they have gone.'

'No!' cried Orlaidh. 'It's too dangerous ... they may still be there.' But, heedless, Murtagh was off, not even waiting for Fionn who shouted that he would go with him.

Cutting across the island, away from the smoking ruins of his home, Murtagh came at last to the hill beyond which he had seen the Land Leapers' boats. Nearer the cliff edge, he dropped on his tummy and stealthily crawled forward. When he looked over, his heart missed a beat. For there in the bay was one long-boat, apparently deserted.

A shadow fell across the turf at his side.

'Get down, Fionn,' he whispered. 'One boat is still there.'

But the hand that took hold of his shoulder was not that of his cousin!

2 Captured!

Murtagh was pulled to his feet and found himself facing the giant Land Leaper at whom he had thrown the eel spear during the struggle for the ladder at the tower. Long red hair and beard covered the stranger's shoulders and chest, and he still wore the helmet with wings and a tough jerkin of hide and leggings of the same material. His arms, which to Murtagh seemed as thick as tree trunks, were bare except for bracelets of gold. Around his waist was a plain belt of hide and from it, in a beautiful scabbard decorated with glistening stones, hung a short sword.

'What have we here, then?' said the man in a thick gutteral voice, as Murtagh struggled like an eel. 'A boy who thinks he can steal my boat, perhaps?'

'Let me go! Let me go!' shouted Murtagh, beating on the man's broad chest.

The man laughed and held Murtagh out at arm's length, his legs kicking vainly in the air. He noticed suddenly that a rough bandage was tied round the raider's right shoulder, and the man followed his gaze.

'I think we have met before,' he said, 'and a boy who can throw a spear that makes Erik Redbeard lose his battle-axe is a better prize than a few sheep — they breed you brave in this misty land.'

So saying, the man started off down the cliff path towards the bay, still holding young Murtagh in a tight grip. As the path narrowed, Murtagh saw a chance of escape. Erik Redbeard was so big that he filled the pathway, which went down the cliff-side in a zig-zag fashion. All of a sudden Murtagh kicked him in the side of his leg as hard as he could. Erik Redbeard stumbled and, clutching at the turf, released his grip on the boy.

Murtagh avoided his outstretched hand, and in so doing tripped. The next moment he was rolling down the pathway towards the strand. The last thing he remembered was the sand reaching up to meet him.

He woke up feeling very sick and sore. His head ached, and when he tried to move he discovered that his arms were tied. What had happened, and why was his uncle's croft rocking so much? Then, in a flash, all that had happened came back to him — the raid, the escape to the round tower, his meeting with the giant Land Leaper above the strand. As his eyes became accustomed to the darkness, he realized that he was out of doors — he could see a few faint stars high above him — lying on something that rocked and rolled gently. He was in the raiders' longboat!

As he tried to raise himself, he was aware of a figure standing a few feet away.

'So, the little spearman has woken,' said Erik Redbeard. 'I think we are now far enough from land to release your bonds. You have slept a long time, but you Irish boys seem to have thick skulls. You will make a good slave for Erik Redbeard.'

'I am no one's slave!' said Murtagh furiously, as the raider cut the rope which had bound his arms. He tried to clamber to his feet, but his head still ached and he felt dizzy.

'Drink,' said Erik Redbeard, handing him a bladder of water. 'You will need your strength in the days to come.'

Murtagh thought of refusing. But his mouth was so parched that he took the bladder and gulped down the cool water. 'Where are you taking me? Who are you?' he said.

'I have told you, little spearman,' said the raider with a mighty laugh. 'You are now the slave of Erik Redbeard. Now we go to the land they call Northumbria, to see whether we have a better catch than we made on your island of monks and children. Although I am not so sure you were not the best catch since we put to sea. I have yet to find a Saxon pup who fights so well.

'And then I think we shall take you to the lands of the north, to show my brothers what a fine little slave I have found. In time, perhaps, we shall make a Viking of you.'

'A Viking?' said Murtagh. 'What is a Viking? You are a raider ... a robber ... a Land Leaper!'

'Ho!' said Erik Redbeard. 'So that is your name for us, is it? Land Leaper? Not such a bad name, for we have leaped out of the sea at the land of the Saxons, and I think it will not be long before we leap again at your own country.'

'Not while King Aodh Oirdnidhe is alive,' said Murtagh stoutly. 'He will soon drive you back to the lands of the north, or wherever it is you come from.'

'Aodh Oridnidhe, eh?' said Erik Redbeard, 'I have heard of this king of yours who bites his fist ... as you see, I can understand your Irish tongue. We have taken many Irish priests in our visits to the Saxon lands. The younger and stronger I did not always slay. They make good slaves and teach me another language, which will be useful when I am king instead of your fist biter!

'So your king will drive us away? And how will he chase us if he has no ships? You see, I know that, too, and how your little kings quarrel among each other. We have no kings in Norway but ourselves — the men of the creeks who bow the knee to no man and who follow no one but the captain of their longboat, such as Erik Redbeard.'

'Where are the other boats?' asked Murtagh who, despite the fact that he was a prisoner with an uncertain future, could not help being impressed with this red-bearded giant. Except for Donal Mór, the strongest man on Rathlin Island, he had never seen anyone like him.

But, even as he thought of Donal Mór, who for all he knew might now be dead of his wounds, young Murtagh felt tears welling into his eyes. He was a prisoner, a slave! Would he ever see his uncle and aunt, his cousins and neighbours, or Brother Padraig again? Like many of his fisherfolk neighbours, he could not swim, and, even if he could, he knew how dangerous the sea could be. Nor could he tell how far from land he was at the moment. The Viking had told him that he had slept for a long time, the result of his fall, and now it was dark again.

'Viking warriors do not blubber,' said Erik Redbeard. 'You will sleep again and then you shall have your first lesson in how a Viking lives.'

Taking up a rough cloak that lay on the deck, he flung it around Murtagh and moved away. Soon Murtagh could hear him talking in a strange language, although he could only make out the dim shapes of other men. He

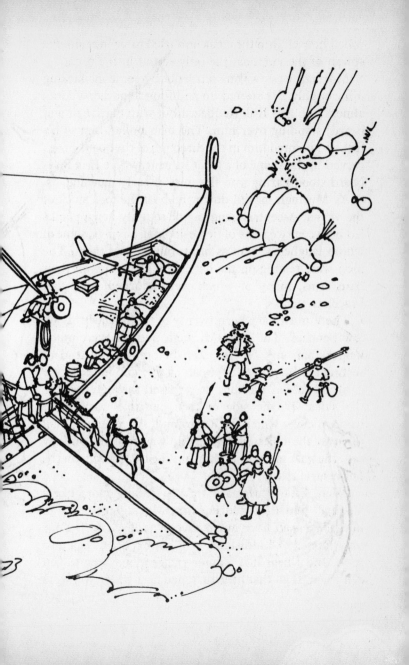

rolled himself into the cloak and tried to sleep again, the splash of the longboat the only sound in the night.

Murtagh was awoken suddenly by someone kicking him roughly. He started up and found another Viking, almost as big as Erik Redbeard but with black hair and beard, standing over him. The man pulled him to his feet and pointed him in the direction of the boat's prow, carved in the shape of a great serpent, where Erik Redbeard stood gazing into the mist of early morning.

As Murtagh moved down the boat, he took stock of the vessel. A central gangway of roughly hewn planks led between two rows of fierce-looking Vikings, some of whom laughed at him as he stumbled past them. The men were resting on the oars, dew glistening on their bare arms, many of which were adorned with gold bracelets.

There must have been twenty of them, all sitting on low benches. The oars, Murtagh noticed, were much longer than any he had seen before, and instead of resting on the side of the boat, as they did in the larger fishing boats of Rathlin, they passed through holes in the sides. To the side of each oar-hole was a little wooden cover which, he was to find, swivelled on a nail to cover the holes when the ship was powered only by sail, the vast sail that hung from the cross-beam on the tall central mast.

'Well, little spearman, are you feeling more like a Viking?' said Erik Redbeard, as Murtagh came up to him. 'We shall have much success today, I feel. Your holy monks of Lindisfarne will not expect us again so soon, and I hear it is a much richer monastery, as you call them, than that little thatched nest where you were brave enough to cast your spear at Erik Redbeard!'

Murtagh had heard of Lindisfarne, a community founded by the holy Irish saint, Aodhan, and much respected by Brother Padraig. If only he could warn the brothers of what was to happen, but the mist hid the Northumbrian coastline, and, in any case, Murtagh had never before been away from Rathlin and knew nothing of the strange land to the east.

'You asked last night about the other longboats,' said Erik Redbeard, as though he read Murtagh's thoughts. 'They have gone ahead to land elsewhere in the country of the Saxons. This will be our last visit before the winter months — we want to have rich spoils to take with us to Norway, to keep us through the cold time when the ice comes and we can no longer take to sea. There will be great feasting when we meet again and, who knows, we may find some of your countrymen to keep you company.'

As he spoke, a faint outline of coast appeared through the drifting mist. As the ship edged slowly towards it Murtagh could seek a bleak shore, not unlike the strand at Rathlin, but without the high cliffs.

Taking Murtagh by the shoulder, Erik Redbeard passed through the alleyway of oarsmen to the back of the boat, where another Viking held what looked like a large oar but which, in fact, was fixed to the starboard side like a great rudder. Erik took the man's place as, very gently, the boat drifted towards the shore.

But as he looked shorewards, his expression changed. 'By the god Thor,' he shouted, 'we have missed Lindisfarne! You see, even a Land Leaper, as you call us, can make a mistake when the sea gods call up such a mist.

But I promise you shall see a better sight than on your own little island yet. Row, oarsmen, row! The wind has forsaken us!'

Down into the still sea plunged the oars, and with Erik Redbeard steering, the ship skimmed inland. The mist cleared and Murtagh saw a deserted beach leading up to a rock-strewn hill. Suddenly the longboat scraped against shingle.

'Akkeri! Akkeri!' shouted Erik Redbeard, and the *akkeri,* or anchor, splashed into the sea. In an instant, the oars had been pulled from the holes and placed across the little benches. The crew rose to its feet and, to a man, leaned across the gunwales of the boat and unhooked a series of rounded shields, which glinted with sea-spray in the early morning light.

'Come, little spearman,' said Erik Redbeard as, catching Murtagh by the arm, he jumped into the sea and, knee-deep, waded to the shore. Murtagh shivered in the ice cold water which came to his waist.

'Never mind, little spearman, you will soon dry yourself at the flames we will light!' said the Viking.

They were the first to reach land, and as they waded ashore Murtagh made a daring resolve. He would make another escape bid! This time, though Erik Redbeard still held his arm in a light clasp, there was no cliff path to hinder him.

'Now or never,' thought Murtagh grimly, as summing all his energy he hit the Viking as hard as he could.

Erik, unprepared for the attack, let go of his arm for a second, long enough for Murtagh to sprint towards the rocky hillside. There was a roar from the Vikings, but he never looked back. Although he still felt very wobbly from the voyage — it was his first, it must be remembered — he said a quick prayer to the great St Columba, patron of his island, and ran as never before. Twice he tripped. Twice he thought he felt the breath of Erik Redbeard on his neck. Then at last he reached the hillside, stumbling on the wet boulders, never daring to look behind him.

He tumbled over the top of the hill, and before him saw a narrow track, little more than a pathway between sand dunes. Down this Murtagh ran for his life, not thinking of where he was going, wanting only to find someone and warn them of the attack to come. He did not stop to think that he had never met a Saxon, and that, for all he knew, he could be slain as a Viking himself.

The mist still hung in patches above the dunes which gradually gave way to tussocks of heather, then to springy turf, finally to a stunted wood into which Murtagh fell, breathing heavily and utterly exhausted. There was no sound of pursuit, and for a second or two he lay still, trying to regain his breath. Then he heard voices and an occasional snuffling sound — the sort of noise a horse makes. It couldn't be the Land Leapers! It was coming towards him from the land, rather than the shore.

The mist cleared to reveal a group of horsemen ambling their way towards the shore. Murtagh saw at once that two or three of them were dressed like the monks of Rathlin, while another, who rode slightly to the front of the group, had long greying hair, a clipped beard and a gold band around his forehead.

As the party drew away from him, Murtagh realized he would have to act immediately. 'At least there are holy men there,' he thought to himself. Leaping to his feet, he ran towards the riders.

'Vikings! Vikings! Land Leapers!' he shouted, never dreaming he would be misunderstood.

The horsemen with the gold band started as Murtagh shouted. His horse, frightened by this sudden vision, reared, pawing the air with its forelegs, and had not one of the monks grabbed the reins the rider would have fallen from the saddle.

Another rider, dressed in a leather jerkin and holding a long spear in his right hand, moved his horse forward quickly and would have speared Murtagh had not the leading monk cried out in a language Murtagh knew well, 'Stop ... it's only a child!'

The man with the gold band, still trying to control his nervous horse, answered the monk crossly, also in Latin, a language Murtagh had been taught by Brother Padraig.

'Who is this? Who dares to stop the King of Northumbria?'

Once more Murtagh felt himself lifted by his shoulder as the spearman took hold of him.

'Father ... Father...,' shouted the boy. 'The Vikings are behind me! There are twenty of them and there are other boats landing!'

'Vikings? Pirates?' said the monk, and turning to the man with the gold band, said, 'My Lord King, I know not where this little messenger comes from, but by the sound of his Latin it's from my own land. There are few of us and, if what he says is true, we have been warned just in time. Child, do you speak the truth?'

'I was captured,' gasped Murtagh, wriggling in the soldier's grasp — he was becoming rather annoyed at being picked up by his shoulder all the time. 'They attacked my island, Rathlin, and carried me here.'

'Rathlin? *Rechru*?' said the monk, using the Latin name of Murtagh's island. 'Then you will know Brother Padraig and Brother Lorcan?'

'Yes! Yes!' cried Murtagh, conscious that time was ebbing away. 'They are safe. We took refuge in the bell-tower. But the Land Leapers are behind me ... I escaped on the shore, but they cannot be far away.'

'Lord King,' said the monk, 'we must turn back for help. We shall bring the boy with us,' and, so saying, he freed Murtagh from the spearman's clutches and lifted him on to his own horse.

'I will not be frightened by a child,' said the King snappishly. 'Let us go down and see what lies on the shore. How could a mere boy have escaped from those pirates? I smell a lie here. How he came to our shores I know not, but I think, Abbot, that there is no truth in his tale.'

As he spoke, the mist cleared and, in the distance, down the sandy track appeared Erik Redbeard, seeming taller than ever, and behind him the rest of the Land Leapers.

'I think he spoke the truth after all,' said the Abbot, once again taking hold of the King's reins and wheeling his horse about. 'We are no match for these Vikings, and Northumbria cannot afford to lose a third king in ten years. Come, King Osred, we must go back.'

The party cantered off into the stunted forest, which

eventually led to a vast expanse of moorland. Across this they rode until Murtagh saw ahead a small group of stone buildings, one or two of which were thatched like the monastery on Rathlin, although the largest building was much bigger than Brother Padraig's church. A wall of loose stone surrounded the building, and as the group cantered through the gateway Murtagh noticed that other men with long spears ran towards them.

'Be ready, the Land Leapers have returned!' shouted the Abbot, who seemed to Murtagh to have more authority than the King.

Although Osred was the first king he had ever seen, he felt rather disappointed in him. Osred of Northumbria was nothing like Murtagh's idea of Aodh Oirdhnidhe, except, perhaps, for the gold band around his forehead. To Murtagh he looked as sulky as his cousin Fionn, the time that Uncle Aonghus had refused to take him fishing because Fionn had forgotten to take a message to Brother Padraig; instead he had sat half the night listening to Donal Mór's tales of the high king's battles, long ago.

The guards rushed to close the heavy wooden gate. The horseman dismounted and, with Murtagh, went into the large building. It was deserted except for two or three serving-men, who fell to their knees as the King entered. Osred ignored them and walked quickly to a rough oak bench at one side of the hall, on which stood a number of goblets and finely made wine jars. He filled one of the goblets with wine and drank it off at once.

'Well, my Lord Abbot, what do you suggest we do now?' he said, glaring at the monk. 'This mysterious boy may have warned us ... but how do we know that he is

not a spy who will escape when he has the chance and tell his pirate friends of how poor an army the King of Northumbria has. Old monks and a few guards! Hah!'

'If the King had made peace with Offa of Mercia, we might have stood a chance againt these raiders,' said the Abbot angrily. 'As it is, Lindisfarne has been sacked once, and there have been sightings of fiery dragons in the sky too often for the peace of mind of your people.'

'Offa of Mercia might well have been a great king once, but he is dying,' snapped the King. 'You, boy, what does your own king think about these raiders?'

'Brother Padraig was going to warn him, when I was captured,' said Murtagh.

'Brother Padraig?' The King took another draught of wine. 'I know nothing of Brother Padraig, although my Lord Abbot here seems to recognize his name. Well, Lord Abbot, what are we to do?'

'The raiders have never before come inland,' said the

Abbot. 'I suggest that we gather what forces we can and drive them back into the sea. I may be a man of the church, but I think that I can still use a sword. How many did you say were in the boat, child?'

'Twenty, not more,' said Murtagh, 'although Erik Redbeard, the leader, is as strong as an ox. But how many guards does the King have?'

'Too few,' said the King, drinking another goblet of wine.

'Our land is going through sad times,' said the Abbot. 'Three of His Majesty's predecessors have been killed by rebellious subjects, and I am afraid that until Northumbria is united we will have no defence against these Land Leapers.'

Murtagh remembered what Brother Padraig had said during the long night in the bell-tower — 'Too many princes who think that they should be the most powerful in the land!' If his own country and the land of the Saxons, or at least the part in which he had landed, were so divided, what hope was there that the Land Leapers might be beaten?

Suddenly cries, panic-striken cries, came from outside. 'The Vikings! The Vikings!'

The King of Northumbria dropped his goblet and turned pale.

'Well, Lord Abbot, it seems the time has come when you can test your sword — and the boy with you. Here, child, take this, and see whether you can fight alongside the monks again.'

So saying, he thrust his own sword into Murtagh's hand. Once again the young Irish boy prepared to face Erik Redbeard.

3 Longboat to Norway

But it was not the Vikings who rode in a stream through the gateway, cutting and hacking at the guards. Mounted on sturdy hairy ponies, the newcomers wore helmets similar to the Vikings, but their hair and beards were fair. Monk and guard fell before them.

'It has happened as I warned the King!' said the Abbot. Glimpsing Murtagh he added, 'Child you have escaped from the Vikings to meet a worse foe — a rebel!'

'If I must die, at least I can die fighting, with a king's sword in my hand,' thought Murtagh.

Within seconds, all was confusion. The clash of sword on sword filled the air. Horses plunged and reared. Men fell from their saddles. The defenders put up a brave fight but all in vain. The horsemen, although small in number, had the advantage of being mounted. As they neared the building, they leapt from their saddles and surged forward.

'Sir Abbot, we have no quarrel with you, except that you keep counsel with this king,' roared one who appeared to be the leader. 'Stand back, and no harm will come to you!'

'I am a man of God, but I also serve my King,' said the Abbot, taking a swing at the man with his sword. 'I have nothing to do with traitors!'

Murtagh dashed here and there like a little bee, hacking at the legs of the newcomers, but dodging a riderless pony he stumbled over the body of a monk and his sword flew from his hand. Landing on his knees, he turned to see the brave Abbot fall beneath a flashing sword.

Suddenly he realized he must escape. Erik Redbeard had spared his life, but he knew he could expect no mercy from these Saxon rebels. He had never ridden a horse, but fear made him bold. As the riderless pony shied from the crowd at the doorway and turned back towards the gateway, Murtagh grabbed his bridle and, in a burst of energy, sprang on to the animal's neck and held fast with both hands to its tangled mane.

'Look, one escapes!' came a shout from behind him, but Murtagh, hanging on to the pony for all he was worth, dared not look round. Out through the gateway he galloped, not knowing where he was going, hoping only to get away from these men who had come to slay the King. The pony headed across the moor and towards the wood of stunted trees.

'I'm going straight back towards the Land Leapers!' thought Murtagh, and very slowly took his left hand from the knotted mane and caught hold of the rope attached to the pony's bridle. As he tugged it, the pony tossed its head to the left, and Murtagh very nearly fell off. But he managed to grab the right-hand side of the rope and pulled hard with both hands. The pony stopped dead. Murtagh flew over its head and landed on the turf.

Once stopped, the pony seemed to lose all interest in galloping and began to crop the tussocks around him. Then Murtagh heard the sound of another rider, and across the moor, from the direction of the fight, came one of the Saxon rebels. Murtagh sprang back on the pony, this time taking the rope firmly in both hands, and kicked the animal's sides. It cantered off at once towards the stunted wood, Murtagh bouncing up and down but at least keeping his balance.

The Saxon was gaining on the boy as they entered the wood when suddenly shouts echoed among the trees and Erik Redbeard and his Vikings seemed to rise out of the ground on every side. The Saxon tried to turn, but too late. Before he could even draw his sword, one of the Vikings felled him with a swing of his battle-axe. The Saxon lay still.

'So, little spearman, you seem to have had no welcome in the land of the Saxons. Have you decided to come back to your old friends?' said Erik Redbeard, as he took Murtagh from the pony's back. 'You have also brought us the gift of two ponies, sturdy beasts which should stand up well to our northern winter.'

Murtagh felt a sudden relief at meeting the Land Leapers again, for although he was as much a captive as before, at least none of the fierce men in the longboat had tried to kill him. In fact they had just saved his life.

'There was a king, and this man,' he said pointing to the dead Saxon, 'was among those who came to kill him and the priests.'

'So the Saxons fight among themselves again,' said Erik Redbeard. 'This will be the third king they have slain, if what we are told by our captives from the place called Lindisfarne is true. My friends in our homeland will be interested. If the Saxons turn against each other, it will not be difficult for Vikings to take this land.'

'Do we go on, or return to the longboat?' asked one of the Vikings. 'We have seen no sign of the other boats since we anchored, and I, for one, do not trust this boy. For all we know, he could be lying about this king-slaying. How do we know that there is not a mighty Saxon army coming towards us?'

'So, Olaf would rather fight monks and children than face an army,' said Erik Redbeard, with a laugh.

The Viking called Olaf turned with an oath. 'No man calls Olaf a coward,' he roared. 'You will pay for your words dearly!'

His right hand moved to the hilt of his sword, but Murtagh sprang forward and butted him in the stomach with his head. Olaf fell backwards and before he could move, the point of Erik Redbeard's sword was touching his throat.

'This is no time for Vikings to follow the Saxons and fight among themselves. You are a fool, Olaf, if a brave one, and there will be time enough to settle our score when we are back in our own land. If we had been there now you would not have tried to draw a sword on Erik Redbeard and lived to tell the tale. For now, I give you your life.

'As for you, little spearman, I am in your debt. You will make a Viking yet, I think.'

He returned his sword to its scabbard and walked towards the dead Saxon. He untied the hide belt, to which was attached a short sword, and presented both to the boy.

'You had best wear this,' he said, tying the belt round Murtagh's waist. 'But if you should ever draw it against Erik Redbeard you will not be spared as Olaf was spared.'

Olaf himself stood up, rubbing his stomach. 'There

may be more than one score to settle when we are home again,' he muttered. 'If Erik Redbeard thinks to win a slave's loyalty by giving him a sword, he had best lie awake at nights!'

'No more of this talk,' said Erik Redbeard. 'I say to you all, now, that this boy is under my protection. Anyone who harms him will answer to me! And now, I think, we will go to test the truth of his story ... if Olaf is not unwilling!'

Olaf growled into his beard, but said no more. Erik Redbeard mounted the dead Saxon's pony, pulling Murtagh up in front of him. Another Viking took Murtagh's pony and the party moved inland.

As they neared the group of buildings, there was no sign of life, and entering the gateway it was obvious that the Saxon rebels had done their work well. The bodies of guards lay on every side, while just outside the door of the hall were those of the Abbot and the King, the gold band missing from his brow. The other monks had vanished, presumably taken by the rebels.

'So this was a Saxon king?' said Erik Redbeard. 'He does not look a noble one, even in death, but a Viking knows how to honour a chieftain in his own country.'

In a short time, the Vikings had gathered a collection of wooden benches, wattles and other material, which they built into a huge bonfire. On this the bodies of the King and Abbot were laid, torches were kindled and thrust into the pyre, which began to blaze. Murtagh instinctively dropped to his knees and said a prayer for the repose of their souls.

'You pray to your God, little spearman?' asked Erik. 'We have different ones, you and I, but unlike Olaf I do

41

not slay your monks because they are of a different faith. The king of the Franks, he who is called Charles the Great, has slain thousands of my faith in the lands of Frisia, as I know from the many who have escaped and come to my own country. You will meet many, little spearman, who have no cause to love your Christians. I am a Norseman born and bred and Norsemen do not, as I told you, bend the knee or change their gods for any man. I trust only in Thor and this....' Murtagh looked up and saw Erik Redbeard touching a rude charm or medallion that hung by a string round his neck. It was carved in the shape of a T.

'It is the hammer of the gods,' said Erik Redbeard, 'protecting us on land and sea.'

'This is my protection,' said Murtagh, reaching beneath his jerkin and bringing out a little bronze cross, which Brother Padraig had given him many years ago. 'It is the cross on which our Lord Jesus died for us.'

'I have heard something of this Jesus from captive monks,' said Erik Redbeard. 'It seems that his own people put him to death. A sad story! In Norway men do not kill their gods.'

'No one should kill anyone else,' said Murtagh, standing up. 'That is what Brother Padraig tells us.'

'In our land, you must fight to survive,' said Erik. 'It is glorious for a Viking to die in battle — he goes straight to Valhalla, to feast with the gods and heroes for evermore.'

Murtagh said nothing. He knew nothing of the gods of the Land Leapers, nor of the king called Charles the Great. For all he could tell, he might be another Land Leaper. He thought it better to say no more, especially as Olaf was glowering at him from beside the pyre.

As the flames grew higher, the Vikings began to load the two ponies with sacks full of weapons, goblets, wine and meat which they found in the hall. The weapons of the dead guards were also collected, and, in a while, the party turned back towards the beach. As they reached the stunted wood, Murtagh turned back. A column of smoke towered up from the courtyard behind them and numbers of large black birds were seen to fly in from the countryside.

'The ravens are gathering,' said Erik Redbeard. 'They always attend a funeral pyre in my land. Perhaps they come now to take your monk and king to Valhalla!'

Murtagh shuddered. He had seen what ravens did to the bodies of sheep that fell over the cliffs on Rathlin, or to ewes that died lambing in the fields. He was glad that the Abbot and King Osred would, by now, be little more than ashes.

Reaching the beach, where the longboat had been drawn up, the Vikings began to load the sacks, stowing them beneath the rowing benches. Two wide planks were lifted down into the surf and the ponies, not without difficulty, were led up them. Ropes were attached to their bridles, the other ends being secured to iron rings in the central gangway of the boat. The oarsmen went to their places, and within half an hour the longboat was moving out to sea. Erik Redbeard stood by the great rudder, Murtagh next to him.

'Say farewell to the land of the Saxons, little spearman,' said the Viking. 'We go now to my home. Stay close to me from now on, lest Olaf seeks his revenge at sea. And when I sleep, be on watch for both of us.'

For two days they were at sea. On the evening of the first, they fell in with the other longboats, the chieftains of which laughed when they saw Erik Redbeard's two ponies and Murtagh.

'A fine catch!' roared one called Ragnar Iron-knee. 'You should have come further north to the rich monastery we discovered!'

Murtagh noticed that the other boats were low in the water, loaded with spoils. Some had fair-haired youths bound to the great central masts, and Murtagh felt lucky that his captor had been Erik Redbeard.

On the second day, about mid-day, a great storm arose. The waves carried the boats hither and thither, and everyone was soaked to the skin by the scudding drenching rain. Two Vikings and one of the unfortunate ponies were carried overboard by one monumental wave, and nothing could be done to save them.

Murtagh felt extremely ill. He spent most of the time crouched at the end of the gangway, nearest the rudder. The oars were not needed now. The fierce wind billowed the sail, driving the boat along at a furious pace, separating it from the others. Murtagh did not care whether Olaf threw him overboard or not. If only he could feel firm ground beneath his feet again!

On the evening of the second day, the wind fell as suddenly as it had risen. The sail fell slack and the oars were taken from the benches again. With two men gone, Olaf said that the slave, as he called Murtagh, should be put to work on an oar, but it was so unlike any that Murtagh had handled that he found it impossible to work. After a cuff or two from the Vikings behind and in front of him, whose oars were foiled by his, he was taken from the bench by Erik Redbeard and brought to the back of the boat and given the rudder.

'See here,' said the chieftain. 'Watch how I work it and do exactly the same. The water is smooth, and we are nearing land. I will take the oar.'

As Murtagh stood at the rudder he saw a thick bank of mist in the distance part to reveal land. It was cold now, and he shivered in his jerkin, even though Erik Redbeard had given him a rough cloak of goatskin. Jagged lumps of ice now floated in the water and also began to gather on the mast. As the longboat neared land, Murtagh saw a coastline of towering hills, covered in snow. There was no strand or beach, but he saw that narrow passageways of water ran inland between the hills.

'The fjords!' said Erik Redbeard, coming to his side and taking the rudder. 'Is there anything as beautiful in your country, little spearman?'

Murtagh could not answer, as he had never before left Rathlin Island, but certainly there was an awe-inspiring grandeur about these fjords as the longboat entered one. The world was white and silent, except for the hoarse cries of ravens, some of whom fluttered around the boats.

'Hah! Our friends have come to welcome us home!' said Erik Redbeard. 'They smell the spoils of war, although do not worry ... you are not ready for the ravens yet!'

Murtagh shuddered again, not altogether because of the cold this time. As the boat passed up the fjord, the rowers began to sing, a deep, fierce song.

'It is the song of returning heroes,' said Erik Redbeard, as he joined in.

Full were they of fighters,
And flashing bucklers,
Western war-lances
And wound-blades Frankish;
Cried then the bear-pelted,

(at this Murtagh looked at the great black bearskin cloak in which Erik Redbeard was wrapped)

Carnage they had thought of,
Wailed then the wolf-coated
And weapons brandished!

Secretly, Murtagh did not think that men who plundered monasteries and attacked peaceful islands like Rathlin were particularly brave, but he liked the sound of the song in spite of himself.

From the distance came the sound of cheering, answered from the boat. The fjord widened into a lake, and on one bank a massive stockade had been built, with wooden jetties leading out into the water. The jetties were crowded with people, cheering and waving, while smoke drifted gently into the clear sky from long wooden houses behind the stockade.

The rowers lifted their oars as the longboat neared a jetty.

'Welcome to my home, little spearman,' said Erik Redbeard.

At the word 'home', a lump came into Murtagh's throat. It reminded him of Uncle Aonghus and the others. This might be an adventure, but would he ever see *his* home again?

46

4 The Great Banquet

As soon as Erik Redbeard stepped on to the jetty, he was surrounded by a crowd of women and children.

'Come little spearman,' he bellowed to Murtagh above the noise of welcome. 'Come and meet my family. You will see much of them in the years to come!'

Murtagh pushed his way to Erik Redbeard's side.

'My daughter, Otta, and my sons, Gunnar and Sweyn,' said the Viking, pointing to three children.

Otta was tall, almost as tall as her father, with long red hair hanging loose, caught with a band across her head. She was dressed in a long woollen robe, with a belt around the middle from which hung a leather purse and a bunch of keys.

'Otta is my housekeeper since her mother died three winters ago,' explained Erik, noticing Murtagh's glance at the keys. The girl, who Murtagh thought must be about sixteen, also wore a festoon of glass beads round her neck and oval glass brooches were pinned on either side of her robe.

The boys were also red-headed. Gunnar was square-shouldered and powerful in build, a year older than his sister. Sweyn, about the same age as Murtagh, was a little shorter than him and slim. Both Viking boys wore woollen tunics with baggy knee-length trousers and leather hose reaching from knee to ankle. Sweyn had a knife carried on a cord round his neck, while Gunnar had a sword, the scabbard suspended by a broad decor-

ated belt — Murtagh learned that it was called a baldric — from one shoulder. Both had tight-fitting caps of wool on their heads.

Otta barely glanced at Murtagh, and speaking quickly to her father moved into the crowd.

'My daughter has eyes only for Gudrun,' whispered Erik Redbeard, as a handsome young Viking clambered on to the jetty with a sack across his shoulder. 'See, he makes her a gift of treasures from your island!'

The boys, however, eyed Murtagh curiously. In fact, Gunnar did not hide his disapproval of the new arrival.

'Since when do slave boys from across the sea wear swords?' he asked his father in a petulant voice, grabbing Murtagh's belt.

Instinctively, Murtagh lashed out with his fists and Gunnar toppled over backwards. In an instant Erik Redbeard stepped between the two boys.

'Stop! You must learn, Gunnar — you too, Sweyn — that this little spearman is no slave. He went to the aid of Erik Redbeard when Olaf thought to kill him. He is to be treated as a brother.'

Gunnar dusted down his tunic and scowled at Murtagh.

'I think you make foes quickly, little spearman,' said Erik Redbeard. 'You must be on your guard against Olaf and Gunnar, but I think you will be able to protect yourself well enough.'

Murtagh saw that young Sweyn was grinning at him, and he grinned back. Murtagh had known what it was to be cuffed by his older cousins on Rathlin, and felt that Sweyn probably suffered from being a younger brother when Gunnar's temper was hot. At least, there was one friendly face in the crowd!

Generally, though, the people in the Viking village seemed uninterested in him, recognizing that he was under Erik Redbeard's protection.

Murtagh followed Erik Redbeard towards the largest of a collection of buildings. They were all built in the same way, with a timber frame and thick walls of turf. As they neared the door two great shaggy dogs came bounding towards them, barking and leaping in the air. They ran straight to Erik Redbeard, and jumped up at him, licking his face.

Erik laughed. 'Ho, Wolf-Bane and Bear-Slayer, are you pleased to see your master again? Get down, get down, you make more noise than the Saxons!'

They entered the long cool building, the dogs sniffing suspiciously at Murtagh's tunic. The roof was curved, reminding Murtagh of a boat turned upside down, and it was supported by two rows of thick posts resting on stone slabs placed on the floor, which was of earth, stamped hard and covered with a layer of rushes. A fire burned in the centre of the building, and along each wall ran a series of wooden benches. Scattered here and there were stout three-legged stools.

Around the walls, rough wooden shelves supported cooking utensils of pottery and metal, and there were many weapons and shields hanging from wooden pegs. Great wooden chests, with iron locks, stood beneath the shelves, and in one corner was a weaving loom — much bigger than those used on Rathlin by Murtagh's aunt and other women. At the back of the hall three narrow strips of cloth were suspended, decorated with what seemed to Murtagh to be scenes of battle.

51

'My wife made those before she died,' said Erik Red-beard. 'See ... they show the great battles in which my ancestors fought. Otta is to make a tapestry of my own adventures, and,' he pointed towards the loom, 'I think you will be in it, little spearman.'

There was a feast that night. The other boats had arrived during the afternoon, and as the sun began to sink — a pale watery sun Murtagh thought it — the men began to gather in Erik Redbeard's hall. The fire, built up on a stone trough which Otta, condescendingly, told him was called a long fire or *langeldar*, burned gaily and the hall was full of the sound of voices and song. Strange, fierce songs, Murtagh thought them to be, the sort of song he had heard on the longboat as it neared the shore. He sat on a three-legged stool behind Erik Red-beard who, from time to time, turned to him with a plate of meat. All the time, though, he felt the eyes of Gunnar upon him and, once, saw the Viking Olaf glaring at him from his place on a bench half-way down the hall. It was not a friendly place, thought Murtagh, while Olaf was around.

Murtagh had never seen anything like the banquet. Occasionally, at home, the people of Rathlin would gather for an evening of stories and songs in one of the little crofts. Murtagh knew by heart the legends of the great king, Conn Céadchathach 'of the Hundred Battles', and of Fionn mac Cumhaill, leader of the Fianna of Erin; and he had heard countless times the stories of the little slave-boy who, after escaping from captivity in Ireland, returned as a man to preach the Gospel.

'I feel a bit like St Patrick when he was captured,'

thought Murtagh, 'and he was a slave for six years!' The idea of not seeing Rathlin for six years — perhaps never again — brought a lump to his throat and stinging in his eyes. He wiped them and saw Erik Redbeard watching him.

'The smoke gets in your eyes, does it, little spearman? But we will make a Viking of you yet! Listen to these songs. I doubt that you have any to match them on your poor little island in the sea!'

Erik Redbeard gave Murtagh a rough translation of the songs, as Viking after Viking added his voice to that of the first singer, making the great hall echo with sound. There were songs about the Vikings' gods — Odin, 'father of our gods', said Erik Redbeard; Thor, with his mighty hammer; Niord, chief of the Vanir, or genii which rule the water, air and clouds. And there were terrible tales of Valkyries, the twelve nymphs of Valhalla; and of Valhalla itself, the great hall of Odin on the hills between the earth and the rainbow, to which every Viking hoped to go after death.

One song in particular stayed in Murtagh's mind that night, a long saga about the theft of Thor's hammer and of how the god had retrieved it from the thurses, or giants. They had demanded Freya, the Viking goddess, as bride for their king, in return for the hammer; and Thor, despite his long red beard, had disguised himself as Freya and entered the giants' hall.

> *His heart within him laughed, the god Thor,*
> *The stern one, when he saw the hammer.*
> *First he smote Thrym, the thurses' king,*
> *Then he slew all the race of giants.*

Murtagh felt as though he was in the giants' hall as he looked round at the laughing, singing, shouting figures. The noise was deafening and the procession of food and drink seemed endless. Slice after slice was carved from oxen roasted on long spits of iron above the *langeldar*. Dish after dish was emptied and refilled from steaming cauldrons of stew. Murtagh noticed that most of the fish had been dried or pickled — he had seen his aunt and the other women of Rathlin busy at this task — but some of the Vikings seemed to eat it raw. The noise, heat and the sickly-sweet mead, which Erik Redbeard gave him to drink in a wooden goblet, made Murtagh's head ache. He longed to sleep, and more than once his eyelids drooped. But he fought against it; he must keep awake and be on his guard, especially against Olaf.

What upset him most, however, at the banquet was the way in which the slaves were treated, even by Erik Red-beard. The fair-haired youths he had seen bound to the mast of one of the other longboats were ordered to serve the Vikings. All were nervous, and many a blow did they receive if they spilt wine or dropped meat on their captors.

Murtagh noticed one slave in particular, a tall black-headed man of about nineteen, about whom he found something strangely familiar. A Viking raised his arm just as the man was to pour him a drink, and the long pottery jug was sent flying across the floor. The Viking cursed and struck the man, who suddenly lost his temper and shouted at him in Irish.

The Viking rose drunkenly to his feet, pulling at his sword.

54

Erik Redbeard saw what was happening and shouted across, 'Leave him, Bjorn, leave him. We have a long winter ahead, and slaves are not easy to come by at the moment!'

The Viking sat down, muttering into his tangled beard, and the slave picked himself up and moved away.

'An Irishman!' thought Murtagh, 'I must speak to him when I have the chance.' Already a plan was forming itself in his mind.

The night wore on. The Land Leapers drank deeply and began to fall asleep on the wooden benches at the side of the hall. Erik Redbeard, flushed with wine, tossed a blanket of bearskin to Murtagh.

'Sleep, little spearman. Tomorrow we go hunting!'

Murtagh took the blanket and curled up in a corner of one of the benches, but he did not sleep.

'I must speak to that Irishman,' he said to himself. 'We must try to escape together.'

At last the hall was full of nothing but snoring. Murtagh had no idea where the captives had been put for the night, but he was determined to find the Irishman. Very slowly he slid from his bench. The hall was cold now, the central fire little more than a red glow. Stepping carefully across the Vikings who lay asleep on the rush-strewn floor, he made his way towards the door. As he reached it, there was a low-throated growl — he had forgotten the great dogs! Luckily he remembered the names. 'Wolf-Bane ... Bear-Slayer,' he muttered, 'good dogs ... lie down!'

One of the dogs continued to growl, and he felt its hot breath on his cheek as it rose from the floor. The growl became louder. Murtagh froze, not daring to move.

Then a voice from behind him, sleepy but commanding, hissed, 'Shut up, dog, lie down!' The dog immediately did as it was told.

Murtagh breathed a sigh of relief. Waiting for a second, hoping that the sleeper had not awoken completely and seen him, he crept onwards to the door. Slowly, slowly, he felt for the iron ring that served as a handle, and pulled it towards him. Outside it was dark, but Murtagh was used to exploring Rathlin at night with his cousins; in fact, his aunt had once said that he had the 'eyes of a cat'. He crawled out from the hall and gently pulled the door behind him, realizing at the same time that he had no idea where he was going. All the buildings seemed the same, although smaller than Erik Redbeard's.

Then he heard a faint sound, little more than a whisper. A voice saying a prayer in the Latin tongue which Murtagh had learned from Brother Padraig: *Pater noster, qui es in coelis, Sanctificetur nomen tuum. . .'* It came from a wooden hut a few yards from Erik Redbeard's hall.

As Murtagh stole towards the hut, a dog barked twice on the other side of the village but there was no other sound. Even the voice inside the hut was now quiet, although as Murtagh reached the rough timber wall he thought he could hear a faint mumbling on the other side. He felt his way along the wall until he reached the door, which was shut tightly and locked on the outside by a stout wooden peg passing through two iron loops, one on the door, the other on the lintel. Gently, Murtagh withdrew the peg and opened the door a crack or two. Inside, the hut seemed darker than the night, but

Murtagh was aware of several pairs of eyes watching him intently.

'Is there a man here from Ireland?' he whispered. There was no answer from the darkness, but Murtagh sensed that there was more than one person there. He repeated the question.

'Who are you?' asked a sullen voice. 'Surely we've done enough work for one day?'

'Don't worry, I am a friend,' said Murtagh. 'Whereabouts are you?'

There was a sound of clanking chains from a corner of the hut.

'None of us can move very much,' answered the voice. 'We are chained to the wall. But if you're Irish, why are you not chained with us?'

'It's a long story,' said Murtagh, staring hard in the direction of the voice, 'but I am going to try and escape.'

'Escape? You will be lucky if you can. If they find you here you will be chained as well, unless they throw you into the sea instead. Anyway, how do we know you are from Ireland?'

'I come from the island of Rathlin,' said Murtagh. 'We were attacked and I was captured. I must get back to warn the High King about these Land Leapers.'

'Rathlin?' said the voice eagerly. 'Rathlin? Then you will know the monastery?'

'Yes,' said Murtagh. 'Brother Padraig is a friend of mine.'

'Brother Padraig? Then you are what you say you are, otherwise you would not know Brother Padraig. He is my cousin. My name is Malachy. I was studying for the church at Armagh and was sent to Lindisfarne when these robbers, these pirates, came. For some reason I was not killed like many of the others — they brought me here as a slave instead.'

'How many of you are there here?' asked Murtagh, still unable to see Malachy who, he felt certain, was the tall black-haired youth he had seen at the banquet. 'Are you all from Lindisfarne?'

'No,' said Malachy, 'the others are Saxons, captured after Lindisfarne. There are five of us altogether, but I doubt that the rest understand what you are saying.'

'Can you sail a boat?' asked Murtagh, the plan still forming itself in his mind. 'If you can, we might be able to put off in one of the smaller boats and try to make Ireland.'

'I have been in a boat often,' said Malachy. 'The monks at Lindisfarne had their own, but it will take more than you and I to steer a course for home.'

'The Saxons could come with us,' said Murtagh hopefully. 'Six of us should be able to manage a small boat.'

'If we could escape and seize a boat, and I say *IF*,' said Malachy, 'we know nothing of navigation. And from what I have overheard from the Vikings, the fjords as they call them will be frozen with ice before long. That is why these robbers never go on the sea in the winter months.'

'Erik Redbeard is going hunting tomorrow,' said Murtagh. 'We will try to get away then.'

As he spoke, he remembered that Erik Redbeard intended to take him on the hunt, and he had no idea how long they would be away from the village. He felt that escape must be tried that night, but how would he release the slaves? He still had his sword — would that be any use? He felt his way across the hut to Malachy's side.

'How strong is the chain?' he asked.

'Too strong to be broken, I fear,' said Malachy. 'In any case, the collar is around our necks, and you could not break it without harming us.'

Murtagh felt the chain which was heavy and thick. He moved his hand along its length until he reached the staple in the wood to which it was attached. Taking his sword from his scabbard, he tried to force it into the staple, then the wood, but both were too strong, and after a moment of effort the point of his sword broke and fell to the floor.

'Listen,' said Murtagh, 'try and work away at the staple with this piece of blade. I'll go back and see if I can find something else with which to break the chain.'

'Be careful,' warned Malachy. 'For some reason or other you seem to be in Erik Redbeard's favour, but if he finds you trying to free the slaves, I doubt that his favour will last.'

'The Vikings are sleeping deeply,' said Murtagh. 'They all drank well at the feast. If I can manage to get one of their javelins, it should be strong enough to force the chain from the wall, but I'm afraid you will have to wear your collar until we are home again, unless I'm lucky enough to stumble over the keys.'

'Good luck, little friend,' said Malachy, as Murtagh made his way back to the door.

'I'll have to put the peg back in the lock,' whispered Murtagh, 'in case any wandering Viking comes along. But I'll be back as soon as I can.'

In seconds he was back at the door of Erik Redbeard's hall. Cautiously, he turned the heavy iron handle and pushed the door inwards. Loud snores greeted him as he slipped inside. The firelight, now flickering from the centre of the hall, showed him a pile of javelins leaning against the wall.

'If I can get one of those I'm in luck,' he thought. 'I only hope those dogs don't wake up again!'

As he reached the javelins, the shape sleeping on the long board nearest to him moved under its pile of wolf-skins. Murtagh dropped to the rush-covered floor and lay still. The Viking coughed in his sleep and turned over. Murtagh lay with beating heart, but no more movement came from the bench. Very slowly the boy stood up and took a javelin from the pile. It was firm, made from seasoned wood, and should be strong enough to force the staples from the wall of the slaves' hut.

Back towards the door he went. There was still no sound from the great dogs — indeed he could not even see where they lay — and once more he turned the iron handle. As he stepped out into the night he saw the dogs and, standing between them, Erik Redbeard, his arms folded.

'Well, little spearman, you decided to take a stroll in the night as well, I suppose?' said the Viking. 'You have brought your spear, too, I see.'

5 The Hunt

The hunting party left the stockaded village at dawn. Erik Redbeard had said no more to Murtagh about the spear, but the boy noticed that the Viking chieftain looked at him from time to time in a curious way.

Murtagh, for his part, was very worried. Not that Erik might suspect his plans — after all, it would hardly occur to the Viking that a small boy could do any damage to a whole village — but that he had failed the black-headed priest and the other captives. They had been waiting for him to return and release them. And, who could tell, if he had not suddenly met Erik Redbeard, he might have succeeded, and they might even now be on the ocean and on the way home! Perhaps it was hoping too much to sail straight back to Rathlin Island, but if the Saxons could steer a longboat to their own shores Murtagh and Malachy might find shelter in an Irish monastery and, in due course, return to Rathlin. There were always boats crossing the sea between Ireland and the land of the Saxons.

All these thoughts jumbled in his mind as the party set off. Erik Redbeard led the way on a shaggy pony, with Gunnar mounted at his side. Six or seven other Vikings, among them Olaf, rode behind them, some of them leading extra ponies on which the wild beasts they had killed would be slung for the return journey. One or two of the ponies carried rough tents made of hide and a number of wolfskin rugs. Another, on which Murtagh

had been placed, had cooking vessels, tied together with a leather thong, slung across its neck.

Murtagh had no idea how long they would be away, or, worse, what would happen to the slaves who had been left behind, in the meantime? Apart from fishing round Rathlin with his uncle and cousins, Murtagh knew nothing about hunting, although from time to time men from Rathlin had crossed to the mainland to hunt the wild deer, and had been away for several days. Murtagh's heart sank at the thought.

The little group rode slowly away from the village, following a stream that ran splashily down from the mountains to the fjord. On either side the land rose, gently at first, but soon they were enclosed in a steep-sided valley. Murtagh, who was used to the roar of the sea at home, had never known so quiet a place. Even the trickle of the stream seemed to be drowned by the silence. Once, far far above him, Murtagh saw the great shape of an eagle, massive wings outstretched against the clear sky. Later in the day there was excitement among the Vikings when a herd of what, to Murtagh, seemed like giant deer appeared on the skyline.

'Reindeer!' said Erik Redbeard, who had fallen back to ride beside Murtagh. 'We should have good hunting today, little spearman.' He looked sideways at the boy. 'We shall see how well you can use that Norse spear ... perhaps. I seem to recall that, once, you did not do badly with a spear in your own land!'

Murtagh began to feel very uncomfortable. Until now, except for the early days of his captivity, he had not been frightened of the great Viking; indeed, there had been times when he felt glad to see him. But now he felt as though Erik Redbeard was watching him, as a cat watches a bird or a mouse before springing, suddenly. The Viking *must* have realized what he was planning with the spear that night. Had he given orders, before leaving the village, that Malachy and the Saxon slaves were to be killed in his absence? Murtagh shuddered at the thought.

'Not cold, little spearman?' asked Erik Redbeard. 'The sun is never strong at this time of the year, but we learn to live with it. And you will soon be warm enough when we find our quarry.'

By this time, the group had reached the head of the valley. Here, the trackway led into a pine forest, dark and sweet-smelling, but away to the right the land fell into a valley far wider than the one they had ridden through. It stretched as far as his eyes could see, until it melted into another mass of forest. In the vast expanse, Murtagh could see herds of reindeer — from here they looked like ants — moving slowly about.

'We are indeed in luck!' said Erik Redbeard. 'I think we should have brought more pack ponies with us. As it is, we will gain a hearty appetite walking back!'

Murtagh suddenly felt hopeful. It seemed as if they might return that day. Perhaps he could try his plan for escape sooner than he had hoped!

Suddenly, he saw one of the groups of ant-like creatures break into a gallop and, at the same time, two or three of the Vikings' ponies began to toss their heads and whinny. Erik Redbeard sniffed the clear air.

'I think we are not the only ones a-hunting today. What think you, Gunnar? Are those grey devils coming down to the lowlands again?'

'Grey devils?' thought Murtagh, as Gunnar nodded to his father and gave a broad grin. 'Whatever next?'

'Don't look so worried, little spearman,' laughed Erik Redbeard. 'Surely there are wolves in your country?'

Wolves! So that was it. Murtagh had never seen a wolf, at least a live one, although the skins in the Viking hall were similar to those brought occasionally to Rathlin from the mainland. But he had heard stories, round the fire in his uncle's house, of how fierce they could be, and how the High King paid men a good price for each wolf head they brought him. He knew that they attacked sheep — and, he had heard, humans — although his uncle's sheep, being on an island, had been in no danger. He also remembered that two of the island men had long scars, one on a leg, the other on an arm, which they said were made by wolves.

One group of reindeer was by now moving steadily towards the pine forest in which the Vikings and Murtagh sat. Erik Redbeard sniffed the air again.

'We are lucky to be down wind,' he said. 'The herd cannot scent us, but they can scent the wolves, which is why they are coming into our trap. A wolf can be a useful creature, little spearman ... if you do not get in his way, and remember to fasten your doors at night!'

The Vikings now began to tether the pack animals to the pine trees and untie the bundles of spears. In a few minutes, Erik Redbeard told five of them, including Olaf, to ride back a little way and then cut into the great valley from the right.

'The rest of you will come with me this way,' he said, pointing to a track that led down through the forest to the left of the valley, 'and we can come in behind the herd on both sides.'

Murtagh gathered that the plan was to drive the herd of reindeer into the smaller valley, the one that led back towards the village, where it would be easier to hunt them down.

Erik Redbeard, Gunnar, Murtagh and two other Vikings rode as quietly as they could down the left-hand track. Murtagh had, for the moment, forgotten his earlier fears. He was actually hunting, something he had never done before, and he felt very excited. Erik Redbeard passed him a spear.

'Even though you did not manage to practice with it last night, you may still get a chance,' he said, with a deep-throated chuckle. Murtagh noticed that Gunnar looked at him in a very curious way.

The track dipped down from the wood suddenly, leaving the pine trees on a broad ridge to the left. Erik Redbeard halted the little column at once, saying urgently, 'We must dismount, otherwise the herd will see us before we are ready for them.'

One of the Vikings was left with the ponies, and told to bring them down when Erik Redbeard gave a signal.

'We must now go on our hands and knees for a while,' he whispered. 'You can pretend you are a wolf, little spearman. If you don't know how to do it, no doubt Gunnar will show you!'

Gunnar ignored Murtagh, pushing past him roughly to fall on his hands and knees behind his father in the damp, springy turf. Another Viking, Gudrun, followed him, then Murtagh who, as he dropped down, turned to look back at the ponies. The face of Ragnar, the Viking who was staying with the ponies, made his heart jump! He was looking at the broad back of Erik Redbeard — and Murtagh thought that never before had he seen such a wicked expression on anyone's face. But he had no time to think about it because, not looking where he was going, he crawled right into Gudrun in front of him. The Viking gave a low oath and cuffed Murtagh's ear.

'Quiet!' said Erik Redbeard, as Murtagh gave an involuntary cry, for the cuff had been hard.

'This is what comes from bringing slaves on hunting parties,' scoffed Gudrun. 'You are getting soft, Erik Redbeard!'

Luckily, the reindeer had heard nothing and were still moving quickly up the valley towards the pine forest. Murtagh could see nothing of Olaf's party on the other side, but he imagined that they, too, were now crawling slowly down the slope.

The herd was now immediately below them, but out of spear range. Erik Redbeard turned on his side and gave two short whistles, the signal for Ragnar to bring the ponies. Nothing happened. He whistled again.

'By Thor!' he muttered, 'has Ragnar suddenly been struck deaf? Go, little spearman, crawl back up the path and fetch the ponies. Be quick, but make no sound.'

Murtagh turned, taking care not to kick Gudrun, and crawled away. The place where the ponies had been left was hidden by a bend in the hillside, but even before he reached it Murtagh knew that he would find no ponies. The spot was deserted!

Suddenly he was frightened. Now he knew that not only reindeer were being hunted that day. He remembered the ugly look that Ragnar had given Erik Redbeard, behind his back, and recalled, too, that Olaf, who had no love for Erik Redbeard, had been ominously silent during the ride from the village. Olaf and Ragnar were plotting to kill their chieftain, of that he was certain! And how many of the others were in the plot? Grimly he realized that if they killed Erik Redbeard, there would be no mercy for him.

What should he do? Return to Erik Redbeard, or go into the pine forest and see if he could discover anything? What about Gudrun, who was obviously in love with Erik Redbeard's daughter — was he to be trusted? Erik and Gunnar were both lying on their stomachs and an assassin could strike at both quickly. His mind in a whirl, Murtagh decided he would *have* to trust Gudrun. The danger would come from the other two.

He stole forward a little way, concealing himself behind vegetation, pausing instantly when he heard voices. Peeping out, he saw, a few yards ahead of him, Ragnar and Olaf — Olaf who should now have been on the other side of the valley — and another Viking, a fierce, short, red-faced man who Murtagh had noticed during the banquet, drinking a great deal.

There was no time to waste! He must warn Erik at once. Stooping, he hurried back towards the downhill path and ran straight into Gunnar, who was coming up.

'Quick! Quick!' he cried, forgetting the animosity between them. 'Your father is in danger. Olaf and Ragnar are going to kill him!'

Gunnar stared hard at him for a second. The boys were standing, or rather crouching, beneath a sloping bank. Then all of a sudden, the bank seemed to move and an enormous wolf sprang through the air. The animal, grey and shaggy, had, luckily, misjudged the distance, but it knocked Gunnar off his feet as it hurtled past.

In a second, however, it was on its feet again and, before Gunnar could draw his short sword, the wolf was on him.

Murtagh did not hesitate. Grasping his spear with both hands, he plunged it at the wolf's hindquarters. The shaft of the spear snapped and the wolf and Gunnar rolled over and over down the slope. There were cries from below — he heard Erik Redbeard's bellow — and a sharp yelp.

Murtagh tore down the path, not bothering this time to conceal himself from the reindeer — what was the use, now? — in time to see Gudrun stabbing at the body

68

of the wolf and Erik kneeling beside Gunnar. Then he heard footsteps behind him and, turning, saw Olaf, Ragnar and the red-faced Viking spring from the track, Olaf with a battle-axe in his hand, the others with drawn swords.

'Ho!' roared Erik Redbeard, 'you are a little late, my friends. Get the ponies ... my son is hurt!'

'Look out!' shouted Murtagh, as Olaf rushed at Erik Redbeard, swinging his battle-axe.

It was Gudrun who realized what was happening. Quick as a flash, he grabbed the dead wolf by its hind legs and swung it at Olaf. The Viking fell sideways down the slope as Erik Redbeard rose to his feet and drew his sword.

'So! We have two-legged wolves here, do we?' he shouted. 'Look to my son, little spearman!'

As Gudrun and Erik Redbeard met Ragnar and the red-faced Viking, Murtagh rushed to Gunnar's side. The boy was unconscious, but apart from long scratches on his face and one arm, where his jerkin had been torn open, he seemed uninjured.

The fight raged furiously for a few minutes. Ragnar and his fellow-traitor had the advantage of being on higher ground, but neither was any match for Erik and Gudrun. A mighty swing of Erik's sword brought the red-haired man to his knees, another left him lifeless on the turf.

Murtagh turned to look across the valley, where he saw the other party of Vikings riding furiously down the slope.

'I hope they are on our side,' he thought, 'otherwise we're finished.' And he murmured a short prayer to the

God the Vikings did not know.

They had forgotten Olaf. The wolf's body had sent him flying down the slope, knocking the breath out of his wicked body — but only for a moment. Ragnar, seeing his friend fall beneath Erik Redbeard's sword, was retreating up the path, Gudrun after him, and Erik turned to his son and Murtagh. His face was angry.

'I was coming back to warn you about Olaf and Ragnar when the wolf attacked Gunnar,' said Murtagh. 'My spear snapped in the wolf...' he stopped short. Erik Redbeard pulled him to his feet.

'I have never doubted you, little spearman,' he said. 'But I fear we are still in danger. How many of our friends can we trust? We must prepare to meet them and die like true Vikings, not like that red-faced coward!' So saying, he bent down to pick up the dead man's battle-axe.

Suddenly Olaf appeared from nowhere. Murtagh had not seen him climb back up the slope and Erik seemed to have forgotten him. Before Murtagh's yell of warning had left his lips, Olaf was upon Erik's unprotected back. Once, twice, he stabbed the great Viking with his sword. Erik swung himself round and fell backwards over the body of the red-faced man.

Murtagh's hand closed round the handle of a sword that was lying on the ground and, like the wolf, he sprang. His blade struck true! It went deep into Olaf's left side as the traitor lifted his sword with both hands, high above his head, to bring it down again on his chieftain. It fell from his hands and down the slope. Olaf turned to Murtagh, a look of hatred on his face, and crumpled to the ground.

'Well done, little spearman,' said a weak voice. Erik Redbeard had propped himself up on an elbow. His face was white and blood trickled from his mouth. 'Well done!' He fell back again, just as the second party of Vikings arrived from the other side of the valley.

Murtagh found himself grabbed by strong hands.

'The slave has killed Olaf,' roared one.

'He has killed Erik Redbeard!' shouted another.

'Kill the slave!' bellowed a third.

A sword was at Murtagh's throat when a cry came from the pathway.

'Stop! Stop! The boy has killed the traitor Olaf! Unless you, too, are traitors to Erik Redbeard, hold your hand.' It was Gudrun.

'Aye — he saved my father,' came another voice. Gunnar weak and pale, had pulled himself up and stood confronting the Vikings. 'The slave from across the ocean is not to be harmed!'

'And Erik Redbeard lives yet,' came another voice, powerful still.

The Vikings and Murtagh crowded round the fallen chieftain. He looked deathly white and stifled a moan as Gudrun tried to lift him.

'I am near to death, my friends, but I am not dead yet. The slave who is not a slave, my little spearman, has served me and my son well. He will be rewarded when we have returned to the village.'

'I doubt that we can risk carrying you that far,' said Gudrun. 'We must camp here and send for herbs from your daughter, that your wounds can be attended to.'

'No!' said Erik Redbeard, with something of his old fierceness. 'I feel I am dying. I command you to take me home. There is much to be settled in the village before I join my ancestors in Valhalla.'

Before long the Vikings had made a framework of pine branches, which they covered with the wolfskin blankets and slung between two ponies, one at the head, one at the foot. On to this, Erik Redbeard was lifted carefully, and with Murtagh walking by his side and Gunnar mounted in front of another Viking, for he was still weak although not badly hurt, the chieftain began his last journey to his village.

6 Death of a Warrior

The sad news had already reached the village, and as the party with its stricken chieftain entered the narrow valley a group of riders came towards it. Otta and little Sweyn cantered ahead of the others — Murtagh's heart was sad for them. Erik Redbeard appeared to be sleeping; in fact the only sign that he still lived was when he grimaced slightly if one of the ponies bearing his litter stumbled over a stone.

Otta and Sweyn turned their ponies and rode beside the litter, Otta staring ahead with the proud air of a Viking princess, Sweyn biting his lips and trying not to look down at his father. Suddenly the old warrior opened his eyes.

'Are we near the village yet?' he asked, and then he saw Otta.

'I fear I give you trouble, daughter,' he said. 'And I feel that your herbs will do little good this time.'

'My handmaiden is preparing a concoction that will heal your wounds,' said Otta, 'and I have already cut the magic runes in the bark and on the leaf of a tree whose boughs bend to the east at the door of your hall.'

'It is the way of our people, little spearman,' said Erik Redbeard to Murtagh, who still walked at the side of the litter. 'You should know, Otta, that this boy from across the sea gained the friendship of our village this day by his bravery.' He paused and glanced at Murtagh, something of the old fire still in his eyes. 'I have called you "little spearman" until now, but what is the name that was given you at your birth?'

'Murtagh is my name.'

'Murtagh,' said Erik Redbeard. Murtagh felt strange at hearing his own name again, the first time since his adventure began.

'Murtagh,' said Erik Redbeard again. 'I think that from this day you shall be called Murtagh Foes-bane, so that all men will know that you slew the traitor Olaf....'

Erik Redbeard broke off and began to cough violently. Murtagh lifted his head gently and held a bladder of water to his parched lips. The chieftain drank and sank back on the litter.

'You will not be forgotten, little spearman, Murtagh Foes-bane,' he murmured, and closed his eyes again.

A crowd stood round the entrance to the stockade, but this time there was no cheering and laughter as Erik Redbeard returned home. They passed round the litter to gaze silently at the dying man, as he was carried into the great hall and laid on a heap of bearskin rugs beside the central fireplace. A concoction of herbs was brewing in a large pot hung across the fire. Into this a strip of rag was dipped and applied to the chieftain's wounds, making Murtagh wince, though Erik Redbeard made no murmur. Otta and her woman bustled round and another brew, foul-smelling, Murtagh thought, was placed to Erik's lips. He drank deeply and, as he lay back into the warm rugs, he said:

'I shall sleep for a while now, but not for long, because there is much to do. Gunnar, where are you?'

The young Viking, his own cuts and bruises dressed with herbs, knelt at his father's side.

'Gunnar, you will wake me when the sun sinks and you will bring the slaves we took in the land of the Saxons to the hall. Now, Murtagh Foes-bane, who risked his life for yours and mine, will keep watch.'

Erik Redbeard slept deeply, but now and then called out in his sleep. Murtagh could not understand what he was saying most of the time, but now and then he gave a fierce shout — and Murtagh knew that he was dreaming of battles, long past. Otta sat quietly at her loom in a corner of the hall. Murtagh was a little frightened of this daughter of Erik Redbeard. She seemed cold and aloof, and almost indifferent to her father's condition.

After a time, Otta left her loom and crossed to the fire. She knelt beside her father and looked across the sleeping man at Murtagh. She gazed at him for a while with a penetrating gaze. Then she rose and beckoned him across to the loom. She pointed to the figure woven in rich colours and almost complete, and she did not have to say anything. Murtagh recognized the warrior at once. In one hand he grasped a great battle-axe, the other rested on the head of one of his dogs, Wolf-Bane or Bear-Slayer. His head was thrown back and his long hair streamed out on either side of his helmet. It was Erik Redbeard as Murtagh had first seen him.

He looked at Otta and saw that tears were filling her eyes. Murtagh touched her arm gently.

'It will look well with the other tapestry,' he said. Otta smiled at him through her tears and, at that moment, Erik Redbeard stirred and looked across towards the loom.

'That is right, daughter, you must smile, Viking women do not show tears, especially if they are the daughters of warriors! Gunnar should come soon, and we have much to discuss.' He shivered violently. 'More wood on the fire, little spearman, the hall grows cold.'

Murtagh collected logs from the side of the hall and piled them on the crackling flames. He was distressed to see a change in the Viking's face, and in the eyes which, usually fierce and bright, now seemed very dull.

Otta hastened to his side and, with Murtagh's help, turned him gently, until he was resting on his left arm. Deftly, she unwrapped his wounds. The smell was dreadful, as she replaced the soiled bandages with fresh ones, soaked in herbs. But Murtagh saw by her face that there was nothing that could be done.

'I think Olaf soaked his blade in poison,' said Erik Redbeard, grimacing as he was turned over. 'I feel it running through me. I should have fallen in battle, not cut down by a traitor! Still, the road to Valhalla is the same, however we take it.'

Gunnar, with Sweyn and Gudrun, came through the door of the hall, followed by other Vikings and, in the rear, chained together, Malachy and the Saxon captives. Malachy saw Murtagh and looked at him anxiously. Murtagh gave what he hoped was a reassuring smile, although he had no idea what was to happen now.

As they gathered round the fireplace, Erik Redbeard told Gunnar and Murtagh to raise him, and to pile more bearskins at the back.

'Now, my friends, listen carefully to what I tell you,' he said. His voice, weaker than usual, was nevertheless clear.

'Soon I am going on a journey to meet my ancestors, where the tales of old battles and victories are told and the old songs of the Vikings are sung for ever. I have sailed the ocean since I was a boy,' here he looked at Murtagh and winked, 'and it is on the ocean that I am going to make my last journey. It is the custom, Murtagh Foes-bane, for that must be your name from now onwards, that when a Viking chieftain leaves this world for Valhalla he is placed on his longboat with his armour upon him and his battle-axe in his hand. And that his horses and dogs and slaves,' here he gave a long look at Malachy and the Saxons, 'are slain and laid on the longboat with him. And then those who are left to fight pile a great mound of soil over the boat and the chieftain, his horses, his dogs and his slaves, who are there to serve him in Valhalla.'

Murtagh felt cold. He was not frightened for himself, for he knew that Erik Redbeard would never harm him — but what of Malachy and the Saxons?

'However,' said Erik Redbeard, 'let it be known that because of the love I have for Murtagh Foes-bane, for the boy I hoped to make a slave and who risked his life for me and my son Gunnar, that there will be no death-mound for Erik Redbeard. He will sail to the west while there is life left in him. His slaves shall go with him, and so will Murtagh Foes-bane, and when they reach the land from where Murtagh Foes-bane was taken they will make a funeral pyre of the longboat, as is the Viking custom when warriors die in a strange land and they will let the boat drift to Valhalla.

'Erik Redbeard has spoken!'

A spasm of coughing gripped the chieftain. Murtagh held a bladder of water to his lips, but Erik Redbeard pushed it away.

'I have no more to say. Let my son Gunnar be guided by Gudrun, and let Gudrun take the hand of my daughter Otta and make her his wife.... And now let a boat be made ready for my journey. I hope your Saxon friends can row well, Murtagh Foes-bane. Their liberty depends on it!'

Murtagh rushed over to Malachy. 'We shall soon be starting on our journey home!' he said.

Malachy's face filled with delight when Murtagh explained what Erik Redbeard had ordered.

'Brother Padraig will find a boat, so that the Saxons can continue to their own land when we reach Rathlin,' added Murtagh. 'Will you explain this to them?'

As Malachy spoke in their own language to the Saxons, Gunnar appeared at their side. He unlocked the chains and threw them in a corner. Turning to Murtagh he said, 'They are no longer slaves. It is my father's wish — and mine!' He hesitated and then held out his hand to Murtagh, who took it. 'I have not yet thanked you for what you have done. I do so now.'

The night was clear and still, stars dancing in the sky, as Erik Redbeard, wrapped in furs against the night air, was carried on his litter to the boat. The whole village followed and watched as Gudrun and Gunnar laid the chieftain on a platform raised slightly above the deck and in front of the central mast. The boat was smaller than the one in which Murtagh had been carried from Rathlin. There was a sleekness about it and Murtagh guessed that in a strong wind it would travel quickly. There were six oar-places — one for himself, one for Malachy and the rest for the four Saxons.

'The wind will be with you after you leave the fjord,'

said Gudrun. 'You will not need the oars.'

Erik Redbeard was propped up on the platform. He called Murtagh to him. 'You promise that you will carry out my wishes, little spearman?' Murtagh nodded vigorously. 'Then all is well. We are ready. Come, children, say farewell to your father until we meet again in the banqueting halls of Valhalla!'

Gunnar, Sweyn and Otta embraced their father and Otta drew from her purse an amulet on a leather cord. She placed it round Erik Redbeard's neck and kissed him on both cheeks.

'You have been a good daughter, and you will make a good wife for Gudrun. Come, no tears, you are a Viking and a Viking warrior's daughter!'

As they turned to leave the boat, Otta paused by Murtagh's side. Reaching into her purse she took out another amulet and hung it round the boy's neck.

'For a safe passage,' she said, and stepped quickly to the jetty.

Murtagh saw that the amulet bore the sign of a hammer — the sign he had noticed on Erik Redbeard's shield. He felt inside his jerkin for the little stone cross which Brother Padraig had given him when he was small.

'This has brought me safe through all my adventures,' he thought, but he was touched at Otta's kindness.

'No more delay!' shouted Erik Redbeard, something of his old fierceness in his voice. 'Westward now, until we reach the land of Murtagh Foes-bane!'

Murtagh took his place at an oar, as did Malachy and the Saxons. Wrapped in a fur cloak, his feet resting on a box of provisions, he bent his back and pulled at the oar. Slowly the longboat slipped from the jetty and out into the fjord. Murtagh turned to look at the long line of flaming torches on the jetty and at the dark shapes of the Vikings.

'Farewell, Erik Redbeard!' came a great cry, 'Farewell!'

'Farewell, Murtagh Foes-bane!' came a cry from Otta.

As Gudrun predicted, the wind met the boat as it was rowed into the open sea. The oars were shipped and one of the Saxons took the tiller, as the others unfurled the great sail. Murtagh went to Erik Redbeard's side.

'Sit here for a while, little spearman, for so I still call you,' said the chieftain.

Murtagh crouched on the edge of the platform and Erik Redbeard looked at him for a moment.

'Murtagh Foes-bane,' he said, 'I think you have grown up quickly in the last few weeks. And I think it will be a long time before you forget Erik Redbeard. But, one day, I feel that you will be a great warrior among your own people and you will need something not only to fight with, but to remind you from time to time of him you call a Land Leaper.'

As he spoke, he moved his hand beneath the bearskin rugs and withdrew from its scabbard his sword, dented after years of battle, but shining still. He handed it to Murtagh.

'I think I shall find another sword in Valhalla to suit me — this is yours. Use it well.'

Murtagh took the great sword in his hands. It was as

long as his own legs.

'Thank you, Erik Redbeard,' he said. 'I will use it well.' He could say no more.

On the third day Erik Redbeard died. Murtagh was kneeling beside him, the Viking propped on his bearskins.

'Little spearman,' he said suddenly, 'bring me my helmet and my battle-axe.' As Murtagh took them up from the side of the platform, he continued, 'Put my helmet on my head and my axe in my right hand.'

Murtagh did as he was told. Erik Redbeard pushed himself up until he was in a sitting position on the platform. He held the battle-axe upright and stared ahead.

'You will not forget your promise, Murtagh Foesbane?' he said suddenly. 'Do not forget the funeral pyre.'

Malachy came to his side. 'The Viking is a pagan,' he said, 'but he is a good man, I think.' And he knelt beside the platform in prayer.

Murtagh felt beneath his jerkin for his cross. He untied the thong from his neck and held it for a while in his hand. Then, bending over Erik Redbeard, he tied it round the Viking's neck, overlapping Otta's amulet.

Erik Redbeard smiled at him. 'I know not your gods, little spearman, but I think they are as brave as you.' Then he leaned back on his bearskins.

'He is dead!' said Malachy, crossing himself.

Murtagh wept.

For two days more Murtagh stood beside the body of Erik Redbeard. The face of the Viking was calm and peaceful, and Malachy had crossed his arms and laid the great battle-axe on his breast.

Murtagh, young as he was, felt very old as out of the mist the coast of Rathlin appeared — the Saxons were good sailors. As the well-known coastline, and the cliffs with their swirling seagulls, came into view, he felt that he had been away for years.

The longboat drew into the shore, Murtagh taking his turn at the oars. It was the strand below the cliff-top from which Murtagh had first seen the boats of the Land Leapers — how long ago it all seemed now. He could smell the turf and hear the bleating of sheep. He was home.

'Now for the funeral pyre,' said Murtagh to Malachy, pointing to the driftwood along the shore. In a few minutes the longboat was filled with wood which was piled high around the platform on which Erik Redbeard lay. Malachy drew from his robe flint and steel, and before long had kindled a fire from a handful of wood.

'Now is the time,' said Murtagh, taking a brand from the fire and wading through the surf to the longboat. 'Tell the Saxons to push the boat out from the strand.'

He climbed on board again and thrust the burning brand into the dry wood around the platform. Soon, flames began to crackle and spit around the base. The warrior lay there, still and lifeless. The flames caught the bearskin rugs and flared up.

'Come down, Murtagh!' shouted Malachy. 'We must push off the boat if we are to catch the tide.'

Murtagh jumped into the surf as the Saxons put their shoulders to the boat. Gently, gently, it began to drift into the sea, the men wading out until the water was around their waists. The tide caught the boat and

carried it away from the strand, flames leaping higher and higher.

'Good-bye, Viking!' cried Murtagh. 'Good-bye — and God go with you!'

In a short while there were cries from the cliffs above, and down the winding path came Brother Padraig, followed by Aonghus, Orlaidh, Fionn, Cathal and, his arm bound across his chest by a bandage, Donal Mór.

'Murtagh! Murtagh! And Malachy!' shouted Brother Padraig. Murtagh turned from the sight of the burning longboat and towards the cliff path. Towards home.

And what a homecoming it was! Orlaidh walking beside him, touching him occasionally as if to make sure he was real. Uncle Aonghus clapping his back. Brother Padraig and Malachy talking nine to the dozen. Fionn and Cathal dancing around, demanding to hear his adventures. The Saxons trailed along in the rear, until Brother Padraig took them by outstretched hand, making them part of the group.

Murtagh the shepherd boy, little spearman, Murtagh Foes-bane, was home. That evening, in the house re-built by his uncle, the people of Rathlin gathered to hear his tale. And the tale is not yet finished, because early the next morning, Brother Padraig crossed the narrow sea to the mainland, taking Murtagh and his sword with him. Their destination was the rath of the High King of Ireland.

The Viking Age

What is known as the Viking Age began in the eighth century, as roving bands of explorers and adventurers sailed from their native Scandinavia. They travelled to distant parts of the world, driven from home by poor harvests, over-population and a natural sense of adventure. They were also traders and, once settled in new lands, set up a commercial network between their colonies and original homeland.

Vikings went as far afield as Constantinople, the capital of the old empire of Byzantium (now Turkey), and many of them joined the Varangian Guard to serve the emperors.

The Vikings were generally men from Norway and Denmark, although our ancestors often confused matters by calling them all 'Danes'. They first appeared in these islands in 793, with a sudden raid on the holy island of Lindisfarne, off the coast of Northumbria; and in 795 they attacked Iona, founded by the Irish St Columba, or Columcille. That year, too, was recorded the first attack on Ireland, at Rathlin; while the coastal islands of Kerry were plundered in 811. By 822 the entire coastline from Wexford to Kerry had been raided.

In England, the real attacks began in 865, when the 'Great Heathen Horde', led by three brothers, Ivar the Boneless, Halfdan and Ubbi, appeared. Within two years they had captured York and over the next ten

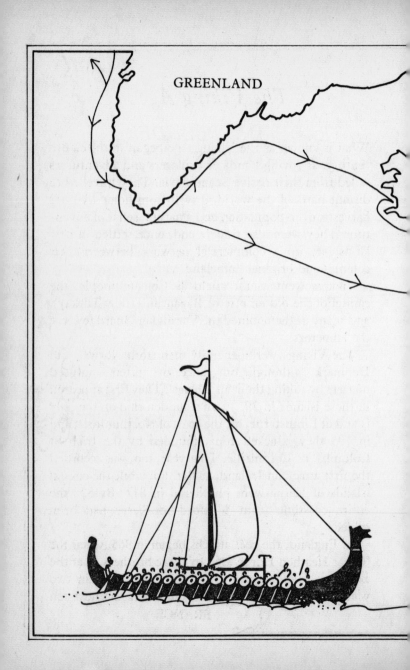

GREENLAND

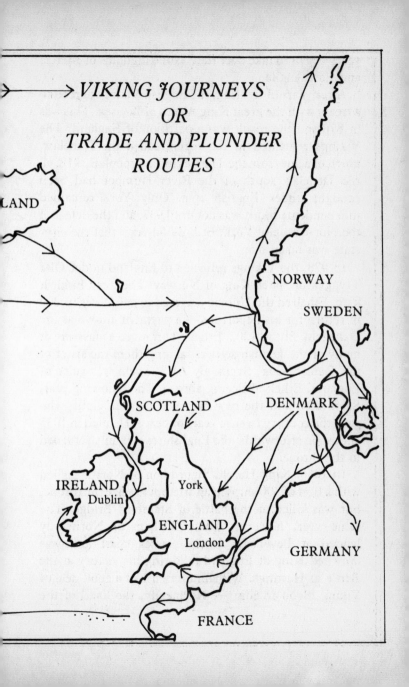

VIKING JOURNEYS
OR
TRADE AND PLUNDER
ROUTES

LAND

NORWAY

SWEDEN

SCOTLAND

DENMARK

IRELAND
Dublin

York

ENGLAND
London

GERMANY

FRANCE

years began to take over the Saxon kingdoms of Mercia and East Anglia.

After years of fighting, the English Vikings agreed to a treaty with the great King Alfred of Wessex. This was in 878 and the result was a partition of England. The Vikings remained in the region called the Danelaw, north of a line from the Thames to Liverpool. By 918, all the Danelaw south of the River Humber had been brought under English rule. Only York remained independent; and it was not until 937, and the defeat of the Norse king of York, Erik Blood-Axe, that the city-state was taken over.

In 978, the Vikings returned to England under Olaf Tryggvason, later King of Norway. The weak English king, Ethelred the Unready, agreed to pay Olaf £10,000 in return for his departure — a payment known as the Danegeld. But in 1002, Ethelred arranged a massacre of many of the Danish settlers, among them the sister of the Danish king, Svein. By 1013, Svein was ruler of England, Ethelred fleeing abroad. The following year, Svein died and the new king was his son, Cnut, who gave the country twenty years of peace. He died in 1035 and, soon afterwards, the English royal family returned to the throne.

In 1066, King Harald Sigurdsson of Norway sailed with a fleet of 300 ships in an attempt to seize the throne, but was killed at the battle of Stamford Bridge. The same year, however, Duke William of Normandy landed at Pevensey on the Sussex coast and was crowned King of England following his victory at the Battle of Hastings. William himself had a good deal of Viking blood in him — Normandy, the 'land of the

Northmen' or Norsemen — had been settled by his Viking ancestors in 912.

In Ireland, one of the fiercest Viking leaders was Turges, or Thorgist, who landed in 830. He destroyed many of the chief monasteries in the country, including Clonmacnoise and Clonfert; and it may have been at this time that many of the round towers — the type of tower in which Murtagh and his friends took shelter — were built, as places of safety in times of attack.

Turges was killed in 846, but in 853 a new wave of invaders arrived, led by Olaf the White, said by some writers to have been a son of the Norwegian king, Halfdan III. Turges had made his capital at Dublin — the black pool — which, originally, had been a crossing place of the Liffey called Áth Cliath, or the ford of the hurdles. Under Olaf and later generations, Dublin developed into a wealthy city-state; and although it was often captured by Irish kings it remained a Viking state until the 12th century.

The most famous champion of the Irish against the Vikings was Brian Boru, who became King of Munster in 976 and High King of Ireland in 1002. He is best remembered, perhaps, for his death at the Battle of Clontarf on Good Friday, 1014, where his army defeated an army of Dublin Vikings and Leinstermen opposed to his rule. But he was an able administrator and a patron of the Church and of learning; and he restored many of the monasteries destroyed by the Vikings.

Although the Vikings were, in the beginning, pagans, worshipping gods such as Thor and Wodin (after whom

Thursday and Wednesday are named), they gradually adopted the Christian faith. Olaf Tryggvason converted Norway in 995 and his son. Olaf II, was to be canonised as the patron saint of Norway.In 1040, Sitric Silkenbeard, King of Dublin, built the Church of St Olaf in Dublin — the site today of Christ Church Cathedral.

The first Vikings had burned monasteries, not because they were attacking Christianity, but because the monasteries were often wealthy, and the Vikings could always be sure to find sheep, cows or treasure there. But after they settled in a new country, and became traders instead of pirates, they settled down. They became more influenced by Christianity, and lived by trading.

Viking houses would have been mostly built of wattle or wood, so very little has survived for us to see today. But towns like Dublin, Limerick, Waterford, Wexford and Cork owe their foundation to the Vikings. Many items from the Viking age can be seen in the National Museum in Dublin, including a set of blacksmith's tools, sword scabbards, pieces from a carved chess set, as well as models of the houses that once stood at Wood Quay, one of the most important Vikings sites uncovered in the city and indeed one of the most important in the Europe of that time.

Notes for Teachers

The excavations at Wood Quay in Dublin aroused tremendous interest. For the first time, the Norsemen, or Vikings as they called themselves, emerged as real people rather than shadowy figures on the pages of a history book.

It all began in 1962, when Dublin Corporation started a redevelopment scheme at Wood Quay, near Christ Church Cathedral, in the heart of old Dublin. Buildings were demolished and the National Museum of Ireland was given the chance to excavate. Dr. B. Ó'Ríordáin dug there during 1962–63 and again from 1967–72. He also dug in the Winetavern Street area, and south of the cathedral.

He dug deep down past the foundations of eighteenth-century buildings, and found in the sub stratum beneath the remains of a large number of structures of all sizes, and no fewer than 30,000 artefacts (*artefacts: a product of human art or workmanship – Oxford Dictionary*). Everything was in a good state of preservation, thanks to the water-logged site.

What he discovered was part of the original Viking settlement, dating from the late ninth to the eleventh century. From the artefacts, it became clear that this had been the craftsmen's quarter. Here lived the leather-workers, woodworkers, metalworkers, comb makers and bone-workers. Among the items found was a soapstone mould for casting the Thor hammer amulet (such as Erik Redbeard wore), and several 'trial' pieces on which the craftsmen tried out various designs.

Before Wood Quay, there had been another important archaeological find. When the railways were being built in the 1850s, a great Viking graveyard was discovered at Islandbridge, just outside Dublin. Unfortunately, the material was not properly excavated or recorded.

The National Museum in Dublin has a splendid Viking exhibition which contains the artefacts found at Wood Quay. A visit is essential for any projects connected with the Viking age.

The Vikings, of course, had other settlements in Ireland. Reginald's Tower in Waterford was built by a Norse king. And *The Vikings*, by James Graham-Campbell and Dafydd Kidd, contains the following intriguing paragraph:

> The Norwegians were also prominent in the North Sea and Atlantic and their most important trading settlement in this area must have been Dublin, a Scandinavian foundation that was exceptionally active and successful in the tenth and eleventh centuries, as recent excavations have shown. Dublin was the focal point on the western trade-routes that linked the Atlantic islands with Scandinavia and western Europe. Its wealth supported craftsmen and artists of many kinds. From about 997 it had its own mint, the first in Ireland. Other important towns founded by the Scandinavians in Ireland were Cork and Limerick, but no traces of these have yet been found below the modern cities.

Who will discover the lost Viking cities of Cork and Limerick?

Suggested Projects

— Is it important to preserve our past? Should the Wood Quay site have been preserved as a Viking museum, or built over?

— Links between Irish Celtic art and Viking art.

— Ireland at the time of the Viking raids; differences between their way of life and ours.

— The Vikings are always portrayed, in Irish history, as barbarians. Were they? Did they contribute anything to the development of the Irish nation?

— Contrast the two great migratory trails of early times; Irish monks east to Europe to spread Christianity, the Vikings west to plunder.

— Shipbuilding; development of the Viking longboat and the Irish currach.

— Song and saga; differences between the Viking saga and Irish epic poems.

Bibliography

There is a growing collection of books dealing with the Vikings. Here is a list of some of the most important. Some are available in bookshops; most should be in your local library. Those marked with an * are particularly suitable for children.

Birkett, Alaric: *The Vikings*. Hulton

Brøndsted, Johannes: *The Vikings*. Penguin, 1965

*Civardi, Anne, and Graham-Campbell, James: *The Time Traveller Book of Viking Raiders*. Usborne, London, 1977

Foote, P.G., and Wilson, D.M: *The Viking Achievement*. Sidgwick and Jackson, London, 1970

Gibson, Michael: *The Vikings*. Wayland

Graham-Campbell, James and Kidd, Dafydd: *The Vikings*. British Museum Publications, London, 1980

Graham-Campbell, James: *Viking Artefacts*. British Museum Publications, London, 1980

Greenhill, B: *Archaeology of the Boat*. A. & C. Black, London, 1976

Harbinson, P: *The Archaeology of Ireland*. Bodley Head, London, 1976

*Hadenius, S., and Janrup, B: *How They Lived in a Viking Settlement*. Lutterworth, 1976

Henry, Bernard: *Vikings and Norsemen*. John Baker

Jones, Gwyn: *History of the Vikings*, Oxford University Press, 1968; *The Norse Atlantic Saga*. Oxford University Press, 1964.

O'Corrain, Donncha: *Ireland before the Normans*. Gill and Macmillan, Dublin, 1972

O'Doherty, Charles: *Early Christian Ireland*, Folens, Dublin

Oxenstierna, Eric: *The Norsemen*. New York, 1959

MacNiocaill, Gearóid: *Ireland before the Vikings*. Gill and Macmillan, Dublin

Marshall, Charles: *Northmen of Adventure*. Smith, London, 1932

Magnusson, Magnus: *Vikings!* The Bodley Head/B.B.C., London, 1980

Paor, M., and L. de: *Early Christian Ireland*. Thames & Hudson, London, 1958

Sawyer, P.H.: *Kings and Vikings*. Methuen, London

Wilson, D.M.: *The Vikings and their Origins; The Northern World.* Thames & Hudson, 1970 and 1980

Wilson, D.M., and Klindt-Jensen, O: *Viking Art.* George Allen & Unwin, London, 1966

The Viking sagas are available in books published by Penguin, Oxford University Press, Nelsons and Dents.

Roger Chatterton Newman

Roger Chatterton Newman was born on St. Patrick's Day, 1949, and brought up in Hampshire. The history of a corner of that county provided the material for his first book, *A Hampshire Parish,* published in 1976.

He writes for various magazines and periodicals, on subjects ranging from rural life to gardening. But Ireland is his first love, and he spends as much time as he can with friends and relations in County Cavan and County Cork.

For Anvil Books, the sister company of The Children's Press, he has written the only full-length biography of Brian Boru, *Brian Boru, King of Ireland* (1983).

Murtagh and the Vikings is set in a period that particularly interests him.

The drawings on pages
92 and 95 are by
eleven-year-old Ian Morris

Hawthorn

is a new imprint for The Children's Press, and will appear on *historical* fiction. *Murtagh and the Vikings* is the second in the series. The first, *A Foster Son for a King,* by Wexford-born Nicholas Furlong, is a marvellously exciting story of the Norman invasion of Ireland, seen through the eyes of the Welsh boy Gwynn, who becomes Dermot MacMurrough's foster son.

Acorn

Adventure fiction for 9 to 12 year olds, in Irish settings.

1 *Robbers in the House* Carolyn Swift
2 *Robbers in the Hills* Carolyn Swift
3 *The Big Push* Joe O'Donnell
4 *Legend of the Golden Key* Tom McCaughren
5 *Robbers in the Town* Carolyn Swift
6 *Legend of the Phantom Highwayman*
Tom McCaughren
7 *Legend of the Corrib King* Tom McCaughren
8 *Robbers in the Theatre* Carolyn Swift
9 *Mystery at Rinn Mor* Jo Ann Galligan
10 *Children of the Forge* Tom McCaughren
11 *The Black Dog* Tony Hickey
12 *The Mystery of the Lost Tower* Jo Ann Galligan

Also by The Children's Press
Silas Rat Dermot O'Donovan
The Matchless Mice's Adventure Tony Hickey
The Matchless Mice in Space Tony Hickey
The Grey Goose of Kilnevin (paperback) Patricia Lynch